Quantum Champion

Expanding Suns (TM), Volume 0

David Aquinas

Published by David Aquinas, 2025.

QUANTUM CHAMPION

First edition. November 1, 2025.

Copyright © 2025 David Aquinas.

ISBN: 978-1969174018

Written by David Aquinas.

Table of Contents

Prologue...1

Chapter 1: Sparring...2

Chapter 2: Mission of Mercy..7

Chapter 3: Summons..15

Chapter 4: Dire News...19

Chapter 5: Negotiations..27

Chapter 6: A Familiar Stranger 36

Chapter 7: Secret Wounds..44

Chapter 8: The Mirror of Flame...50

Chapter 9: One Question, One Boon...57

Chapter 10: A Minor Setback 61

Chapter 11: Words of Power...68

Chapter 12: Beginning to See 76

Chapter 13: Fire..81

Chapter 14: Lightning...85

Chapter 15: Heart's Blood...91

Chapter 16: Cornered 92

Chapter 17: A Secret Revealed...94

Chapter 18: The Grand Arena..98

Chapter 19: The Quantum Champion.. 101

Chapter 20: The Rose in Winter.. 107

Enter the worlds of David Aquinas. To learn more go to:

"Battlefleet keeps the peace, but the Mirrors keep the soul."

-- Altari proverb

Prologue

I, Arkasa Sargosan, sarpan ambassador to humankind have written an orderly account of recent events so that you may know of humans and come to understand them better. Not all sarpans regard humans as prey and I wonder what secrets humans harbor, hidden even to themselves.

In the 500th year since the ascendance of paramani Kashendra Ashastra to the Emerald Dais, to rule all humans in known space across the twelve Great Houses of the Altari republic; humans have been the newest and most suspect members of our galactic civilization which calls itself the Commonwealth of Stars. Bound in a tenuous peace for millennia under the Seven Precepts, the Commonwealth Battlefleet enforces the peace, but the mirrors of the amari, mysterious space-time portals allow faster than light communication among the capital worlds of each race helping bind the civilization together.

In the *Litany of Stars*, short-lived humans are likened to sparks that dance among the flames. Some say that they will ignite a fire that will collapse the galaxy into civil war. For this reason, the human nobility have bound themselves under a code duello to channel their ambitions, the *vendamasthra*, the "game of knives," to prevent open war.

Among humans, the quantum champions, a handful of single combat warriors, enforce this custom, ensuring that peace continues.

But there are always those who follow no code but their own will.

Chapter 1: Sparring

Rory Demaris looked up to see the face he most loved in the world.

The sparring session at the palace gymnasium complex had ended when his partner read his feint. Instead of blocking and counter punching, she switched forms and twisted his right arm, leveraging his weight to slam him down onto his back.

Jade Coriander, quantum champion of her house, one of only twelve in all human space, looking down smiled and told him. "You led with the spear hand when you should have used the knife hand."

He sprang to his feet on the exercise mat. "You surprised me."

"Don't blame me for your lack of focus. Think," she said.

The mat's depression bespoke how hard he had fallen. "It is good to see you again."

"Don't," she said.

"Don't what?" he said.

They walked towards the lockers at the back of the gymnasium. On the way out to the atrium leading to the air car port on the palace grounds, he stopped her.

Twirling a finger around her ear as she dodged, he unfolded a pink rose from his fingers. "See, I conjured this just for you."

"There's no such thing as magic, she said.

"Not even love?"

"I am headed out on the battlestar *Eye of Indra* tomorrow."

Another quick turn of his wrist, another flower. "Marry me."

The flower passed to her hands, her eyes moist. "That isn't how it works in our society, Rory."

"One day you will step down from your post to marry."

"And the paramani will pick a suitable husband," Jade said.

"What's so unsuitable about me? Not blue blooded enough? Seventh son's curse? It's not my fault I don't have an inheritance."

She pursed her lips in a hard frown. "Don't be an ass."

He restrained an impulse to dance around her like an overwrought puppy. "Why not? I've the best transport record in the merchant guild. No shipments lost to pirates."

They stepped out onto the pavilion outside the gymnasium complex. She looked at the sky as if to appeal to a higher power. "You might be a lucky catch someday for the right woman."

Air cars raced by at intervals across the 6000-acre grounds of the paramani's palace on the planet Coriander, one of the twelve major houses of the Altari republic.

" I don't want any other women."

"I don't think you know what you want, Rory."

"So, what if I like a game of snapdragon now and then? Make friends and influence people. I haven't looked at another woman since I can remember."

"Drinking clouds your memory, I imagine."

"Maybe. But I'm clear about you, Jade."

Cypress trees bordered the broad boulevard, where civilians walked towards their duties at the various buildings of government and administration.

A contrail of a hyperloop transport flared in the stratosphere at the top of a loop. A bright star hung near the horizon. In the clear morning air, the light shone steadily at the spaceport.

Jade glanced back at him. The conversation always ended badly. The obstacle to his desire had been set in place by a rash word as a youth, and now that he was more circumspect, there was no remedy.

Rory pressed his case. "My father married for love, you can too,"

"Your house is a minor one, and proscribed since your father lost his duel."

"You bloody nobles. Why do you all look down your noses at everyone else? "

"Look what happened to your father. Do you want a repeat of that?" Jade said. Putting a fist to her head, she shut her eyes. "Why do we always do this to ourselves?"

Rory turned his face away. The Altari republic gave justice based on rank. There could be no recourse. Only a duel could satisfy honor after Rory blurted out the insult, and his father had lost, and triggered the reprisal that made him and his mother a pariah. If Jade's mother hadn't defied another house to show them mercy, what would have become of them? It didn't stop his mother from dying of grief. And now he felt as if he carried her grief with him and it would never end.

He sighed. "Why join a Battlefleet unit? Isn't your job to protect security at home?"

She shrugged. "Home has a wide definition for house politics. I'm just following your hunch."

The Altari Republic ruled mankind across through twelve fiefs governed from a dozen worlds and many more tributary colonies, yet the billions of humans were only a fraction of the sapients that made up the vast galactic civilization of the Commonwealth of Stars.

"My hunch?" he said.

"About space-time distortions affecting the jump lanes."

His heart pounded. Jade might be the paramani's right hand on Coriander, but she hadn't traveled the space lanes like he had, not to mention smuggling. "That's just a theory. Scoutfleet can check it out and you can examine the report."

"House Zayan is mucking up the administrative chain with red tape and bureaucratic obstacles. I have to see for myself."

"By all the seven mirrors, Jade. Pirate raids are boiling on the frontiers, some of it sarpan, stay home and let underlings like me handle it."

The sarpans were the warlike saurian aliens who regarded all other sapients as potential prey. Their government abided by the Commonwealth Articles, but their pirates didn't for the same reason human ones didn't. It was a matter of debate among the more pacifistic races which species was the most bloodthirsty. Yet humans were the newest and most suspect race to join the Commonwealth. Other aliens seemed to fear them more than being eaten by sarpans.

"I'm taking the *Cormorant* out to the Arch Radiant." Rory said.

"Oh? What trade score are you planning this week?"

"I'm taking a shipment of vaccines to Angyran Secunda."

Jade shook her head. "It can't be worth the risk. Better for a house guard unit to do it."

"Sending the militia won't cut it."

"It will still be a Battlefleet warship."

"They won't dispatch a big enough ship for the risk, and the *Cormorant's* got faster legs since I paid the filtrigs for her overhaul."

"The *Cormorant* is still a bucket of junk. I'm sorry, just a merchantman," she said.

He whistled.

"You didn't bootleg illegal hardware off the filtrigs, did you?"

Plying a thin smile. "It's goya work I needed."

Her eyes widened. "You didn't?"

"I did. They have nothing against defensive weapons."

The filtrigs, humanoid of rat like demeanor and intrepid engineers vied with the shy goya, who hid within their clown like methane environmental suit. The two species competed for dominance in specialized starship technology.

"Someday, Rory, your deviousness is going to get the better of you."

"Jade don't go. I have a bad feeling about this."

She patted him on the cheek. "Don't be superstitious, you just want to seduce me."

He gripped her wrist and pulled her hand to his lips to kiss it. "True but marry me first and we'll make our own dynasty."

She pulled her hand away and sniffed. "Incorrigible romantic."

"I just know what I want."

She sighed. "Let a House guard unit take the vaccine and come with me to investigate your bogeyman theory."

"It's just a hunch. Let the Scouties help Battlefleet do their investigation, and you can come help me deliver the vaccine."

"Be well, Rory Demaris ni Coriander."

The formality was a dismissal. He stared into her green eyes, taking in the sight of her.

She turned and walked away.

Chapter 2: Mission of Mercy

He met his helmsman, navigator Aleksy Joort, at the landing zone for the port shuttle a day later. A commoner, tall and thin, he possessed the best mathematical mind in the merchant guild and would have been his executive officer if Altari law permitted it.

"Good day, my lord," Joort greeted him.

"Mr. Joort," Rory said, looking about to spot cameras. The ones he could see were few.

A tall woman with the bearing of a Valkyrie and a sharp chin strode up. She wore a mercantile guild service dress uniform, tan and maroon, with a broken star and comet shoulder flash. "My credentials, Rory ni Coriander." She presented the data pad.

He frowned. "Thanks for joining on such short notice, XO." Rory only trusted Joort as permanent crew, and rotated bridge crews depending on the delicacy, or legality, of the run.

"Delta Zayan, Captain."

Typical Zayan attitude. "How did you get the guild to break its rules?" he said.

"No breach of custom, sir. Technically, I am Delta Zayan ni Coriander."

The Altari hold to matrilineal succession even if power is shared by cach paramani and her war leader. Delta Zayan had not given up her legacy but had married a house Coriander noble. Was it arranged or for love? Who could tell? He was biased against Zayan motives, not without evidence from past run-ins at their custom houses.

"Ah." He wondered who had married into her line.

Her eyes narrowed.

He felt remorse at his prejudice. Her position wasn't all that different from his. "Mr. Joort has briefed you, I assume.

She sniffed. "He is a very efficient man."

"Just another peon, my lady," Joort said. "Efficiency is my lifeblood."

Joort deserved better than his status afforded. The Altari government's near caste system chafed him. The same system that kept Rory from marrying Jade. In a sense, it wouldn't be legal, and he had never convinced her to go rogue just to be with him. Social norms had shaped both of them, and he dreamed of a world where just being yourself was enough to gain happiness.

"Captain?" Joort's voice brought him back into the present. Delta's face was neutral, but her eyes alert, taking the measure of him.

"Fine, we've loaded the vaccine. Let's go."

"Aye, captain," they answered in unison.

A week into the jump, Rory sat in the captain's chair of the *Cormorant*, outward bound for a remote fief with a vital supply of vaccines.

His ship was transiting a wormhole tunnel three bands down in n-dimensional space, or n-space, as the shorthand went for the collection of infinite overlapping space-time continuums above and below our own.

The deck plates had worn depressions from decades of boot traffic before he acquired it from a House Rialto broker. He replaced the worst of the plates as safety hazards and covered the main corridor floors with plastomer grids to save cost.

The bulkheads were bare of elegant plasteel panels to make things look pretty. The *Cormorant* had the speed of a falcon, if without talons to match. Mostly, she was a trader, after all.

"My Lord Captain," Mr. Joort intoned.

He rolled his eyes. "On board, Rory will do, Alex. More efficient."

"Very well, two syllables it is, My Lord. There is a ripple in the bow gravity wave gradient approaching us."

He leaned forward. "Another jump lane drift?"

"Possibly. Shall I push off our descent for time to analyze it?"

"And then what? We can't linger here, and we can't turn back."

"In extreme danger we could scram the jump," Delta said.

Scramming was not the same thing as aborting a jump prior to entering transit. Crashing through the wormhole sidewall into a random point of interstellar space would delay them too long, and damage to the ship and crew from tidal forces was unpredictable. "Right. Right. By the book then. But remember the colony's need for this vaccine."

Joort reversed thrusters, and the ship's descent slowed. He threw up a holo display, a virtual map of how each layer of n-space mapped point to point. The sensors could only interrogate so many layers deep into space-time, and only within a certain radius of the ship. His filtrig upgrades lent an advantage. Their enhanced spatial gravilinear plot map let him judge his options better than most sensor packages.

Rory tugged on his vest and chewed his lower lip. "What do you think of it, Mr. Joort?"

"Indeterminate, my lord."

"XO?"

"I don't know, captain. Jump lanes have been dicey lately. Scoutfleet has doubled the mapping sorties to keep up with lane drift.

"Yah, well, they missed this one. I wonder how new it is and what caused it? Resume freefall."

An hour later, the *Cormorant* reentered normal space, but there was no colony to be seen.

Nor a local star, just the panoply of stars dusted across deep space.

"Feldspar take me. How long will it take to recalibrate a new jump with the navcom?" Rory said.

"Scanning. Without a local star beacon - ten hours," Joort said.

Rory whistled. "No help for it. Make it so."

Delta chided. "Something is amiss. Best leave the colonists to themselves."

Joort scowled. "What happened to noblesse oblige, and all that rot, hmmm?"

"I'm more willing to give up the bounty than transit unstable n-space. Besides, they did it to themselves."

In a way, the colonists had, violating Commonwealth research protocols about cross species enhancement of function experiments. Rory had paid a substantial sum of his gold quant savings to an orphan drug lab to print up a vaccine against the genomic virus that had driven the cancer rate on the colony up to astronomical proportions. The mutation rate had sped up, hence the urgency of the mission.

Rory wished there were a circle of hell fit for the arrogant bastards who thought they could play God and get away with it. Their leaders had quarantined themselves at the plague outbreak and sent for help. "It's not the citizens' fault their leaders screwed up." Especially since the citizens didn't really get much of a say who ruled them. "I'll buy you a drink when we get home from saving plague victims."

"More drinks, I expect, than that," Joort said drily.

"Once we have a navigation solution, we'll launch a courier drone to the nearest Scout Depot for relay to a Mirror station. Let the Scouties have more work and know the reason for our delay."

"Aye, my lord."

"Captain?" the XO said. "We are being pinged."

"That's impossible. Who would be exactly here in the black between?" The control board lit up like a Jubilee fireworks show.

Among humans, the Jubilee is celebrated every seventh year on the capital world, Altarsha. Boons are granted by the paraman as rewards for faithful service. It is attended by dignitaries from all worlds of the Commonwealth. Even the sarpans abate their bloodthirstiness for diplomacy on that day.

"XO, have we got us some pirates?"

Her cheek clenched. "Unless it's a rogue Battlefleet unit. I count two ships, a 2000 tonner and a 20K, no missile hard points, must be the tender. The smaller ship is boosting at attack speed and will close in six minutes. Idiots."

"Call General Quarters." Rory ordered.

The klaxon sounded everywhere on the ship. Crew men and women sealed their skinsuits and donned helmets. The security squad broke out the personal weapons allowed to a trader under Commonwealth shipping regulations.

"Hull temperature rising sir."

"Let's hope those goys pacifists gave me my money's worth. Activate the Sheer Field on the closest bogey when it's in range."

"But the fusion core?"

"It's filtrig and can take the load. Burn hot, Alex."

The *Cormorant's* oversize maneuver thrusters, Mark five, mod four filtrig enhanced plasma fusion engines, pushed their g's, and the ship corkscrewed in a maneuver beyond the direct line of laser fire.

"Red line it, Alex. Target a shot on their tender."

"A second ship has launched, Captain," the XO said. "An assault shuttle."

Rory chewed his lip. "Take out the lead ship Mr. Joort."

"Aye, Aye" As the passing corsair maneuvered for another shot, it encountered the goya Sheer Field. Designed purely as a defensive wall against saturation missile barrages, directed orthogonally, its edge disintegrated matter crossing its n-space gradient. The corsair looked intact on the viewscreen for a few seconds then tumbled into halves, one of which exploded taking the entire ship out in a blast of plasma fusion.

Rory grimaced. "Who do they think they are, these peasants?"

"The assault boat is closing. What if they take our ship for their next ride?" Zayan said.

"Such an optimist. Burn them."

Joort tagged the intercom. "All hands, brace for more g's."

Joort executed the burn, and their counter-fire scored a hit on the assault boats engines. Not enough energy against their armor to make a difference.

Proximity alarms rang. "Evasive, Alex."

The *Cormorant* fell back from the line of attack.

The hull shuddered.

"Captain, atmosphere venting on dorsal aft section three." The XO said. The unmistakable sound of mechanical grapples rang the hull.

The XO threw a ship hologram onto the view screen. A dozen red blips fanned into the breached corridor and broke into two groups.

Rory drew his contraband plasma blaster. "Repel boarders! Joort, you're with me. XO take the con."

He charged aft and down on the starboard side, and into the melee between his crew and pirates—not humans, but sarpan raptors. His crew had barricaded them further aft, pinned near the entry breach they had grappled with his ship.

The saurian aliens wore standard mining gear without markings.

"Mercenaries. This doesn't parse. Sarpans don't hire out as mercs," Joort said, ducking under a fusillade of plasma bolts. Metal vapor stung the air.

"Uncreched renegades do. Where's their controller?" Rory caught a boarder in mid jump, shot it in the haunch and it fell over snarling, dewclaws on its legs clawing the air, its elongated snout shaking inside its helmet.

They couldn't just stay pinned until the tender caught up with them and sent more troops.

The bridge signaled him, the XO's voice strained. She reported a party was beating on the bridge's hatch from the corridor, trying to break in.

"Damn all." He left Joort with the main party going aft, took two crew with him, and when he got back to the bridge saw two sarpans and a human in unmarked space suits. One of the sarpans applied a cutting torch to the hatch, actinic sparks flying.

Rory blasted down the sarpan wielding the cutting torch. To his side, the sarpan with open helmet visor, the better to bite when closing, sprang a five-meter distance in one hop to tear out the throat of a crew member as the other one wounded it with a glancing shot from a recoilless pistol that jammed. The crewman backed away from the snarling sarpan, breathing hard as it stalked forward, temporarily ignoring Rory.

Meanwhile, the pirate leader, a human, drew a blade on Rory from a boot scabbard. The knife was a hummer, a counterfeit spire dagger. Though it lacked the characteristic white blazing light that could cleave any matter but adamantine warp core armor, the shear field humming on a steel blade could still cut Rory's hand off in one swipe. This wasn't goya hardware but must have been smuggled from a factory at the capital.

Rory crescent kicked the knife out of the pirate leader's hand and used a spear hand thrust to his throat, leaving him to gag on the deck clutching at his neck. Rory ripped off the pirate's communication device on a pectoral collar affixed to his suit.

A saurian scream reverberated behind him, and he linked the vox box to his suit in time to translate into sarpan on their combat channel. "Avast, you sorry guppies. Stand down for your new master."

They blinked.

When the sarpan pirates turned, the fight ended. The tender that had brought the boarding party and its escort jumped out.

Joort caught up and bound the prisoner, taking him to a stateroom for interrogation.

Rory resisted the impulse to space him and be done with it.

Joort updated him ninety minutes later, while Rory cleaned up after the mayhem, checking the *Cormorant* for damage. "Captain, our prisoner won't talk, but you should see something."

Rory joined Joort. The crewman who had nearly been killed in the boarding action stood watch. "What now?" Rory said.

Joort pointed. "The tattoo there, on his left forearm."

"Former military?"

"Yes, sir."

"I can barely see it."

"The dermabrasion to remove it was sloppy. Broken stars and comet. House Guard."

Rory wondered if his XO had set him up. "Secure him in a locker until we get to port and let's go have a talk with our XO."

The talk revealed nothing. With the usual Zayanite hauteur, his XO told him it was beneath her dignity to follow the post service life of every commoner veteran, and for Rory to go put his head in a raptor's mouth if he expected any more information from her.

Rory admired her for not giving away anything, and strictly speaking, not lying either. He confided to Joort out of her earshot. "I doubt the XO would have barricaded herself in the bridge if she were on their side."

"Never underestimate plots among nobles."

"Technically, I'm a noble too, Alex."

"Yes, and you are an admirable example of conniving skill."

"Well, my conniving street sense wonders if we've stumbled into a vendetta."

Joort recalculated their jump vector, and they made the colony just in time to deliver the vaccine to protect the survivors, and hand over the prisoner to authorities. *Pity I can't arrest their president for unsanctioned gene research.* Justice would have to wait for the afterlife, if there were such a thing. His mind turned to Jade and how to pierce the labyrinth of social class wound about her so tight it seemed impenetrable.

Chapter 3: Summons.

Rory rose up from his pallet, sputtering and choking at the water that had been dumped upon his head as he slept off his drunk from carousing the night before. He wiped his eyes and raked his black hair back to see unsmiling men in cobalt blue dress suits with gold ties. They wore HUD visors that obscured their eyes, and their flat frowns were enough to know he was in trouble. "Rory Demaris ni Coriander", the older one of the pair said, "Your country has need of you."

They gave him enough time to shower and dress. Wearing the casual brown and maroon street gear of a common merchant pilot, he paid his tab to the innkeeper in gold quants. The coins aroused interest from others in the foyer, sitting around on divans relaxing or at table. The decor was jungle and mist in style. Locals came here for reading, and drinking by day, and more bawdy entertainment by night. At present, a few business executives read from data pads or lips murmured as they sub vocally spoke to other parties through virtual commlinks.

At a corner table by a tall vertical window with streams of light casting wavering shadows sat two filtrigs, the alien tinkers humans value for starship drive upgrades and bootleg liquor. Squat and sinewy, they were vaguely humanoid, but with rat like faces and dorsal humps with shaggy fur. Their arms, bare except for gold or electrum bracelets, their six fingered clawed hands held flutes of fluorescent yellow green ambervis. One of them raised a glass as if to toast him. She seemed vaguely familiar, and the splitting headache suggested he had spent the night drinking more than beer.

Rory returned the salute with a nod. His keepers hustled him out the door into an air car that took him to the palace grounds. Coriander's sun was yellower than Altarsha's, and the sky bluer too. Wispy cirrus clouds drifted overhead, and the contrail of a stratospheric transport crossed over them. The air car raced 100 m above ground through an express lane reserved for nobles, then ascended to 10000 meters on a ballistic trajectory.

Beyond the metropolis spread the palace, a sprawling complex of terraced marble and acacia wood, all 6000 acres of it, looking small as a postage stamp from this vantage. It grew rapidly at the speed they were traveling and plummeted towards the ground on approach, skimming towards the Lion's gate. Suppliants and merchants waited to be checked through by house guards wearing service dress blue and gold uniforms. The guards snapped with salutes as they sped through to a broad lane bordered by a graceful white colonnade and branched off to the gymnasium and armory complex.

His escort deposited him into an atrium with a bamboo parquet floor and wood-paneled walls, the room lit softly by indirect glow lights hidden around the ceiling. The far door opened, and his arms master walked in.

This was totally outside protocol. All he could think was that someone had challenged him to a duel and sent her to deliver the challenge. It still made little sense. Unless he had fallen into some other plot, in the rarefied world of court politics.

Cassandra Orvieto, daughter to a gentry family that had served House Coriander for 10 generations, crossed her arms, tapping her foot and looked at him with a skeptical eye. She took over as his instructor after his first sensei left his training when he turned of age as suddenly as she had appeared.

Orvieto wore a loose-fitting black fighting dress that resembled pajamas more than anything else and black slippers with flat heels. "Did you enjoy yourself out there?"

Rory frowned. "Why the coercion?" He touched his aching forehead.

"The *vendamasthra* is in play."

"Politics is not my problem. Did I offend some noble brat accidentally at a card game?"

"The game of knives doesn't care about your feelings, Rory."

"We don't have any training sessions scheduled today."

"You know of the instability in the star jump lanes lately?"

"There's a hiccup in n-space once in a while. A ship with a good navcom and the right navigator can recalculate the gradients and make it home—most of the time."

"The maryana home world mirror relayed a message to Altarsha about an unexpected nova obliterating one of their colonies."

He liked maryanas. The diggers were a friendly sort, and if they looked like overgrown moles to humans, he never found them to be lacking in humor. And their metabolism could out drink anyone except a filtrig. "How old is the news?"

"The scout relay courier arrived thirty-six hours ago."

"You had house security roust me for that?"

"Jade's starship was caught in the wreck. She's just so many atoms floating in plasma now."

"Rory. Rory!" Orvieto said.

Pulled back into the moment, he nodded slowly. "That's impossible." He staggered.

"Pull yourself together, mind like moon, mind like water-remember?"

The martial arts dictum hammered into him from the first day of dojo practice at age six when he first donned a gi two sizes too large for him was not enough to steady him.

"I grew up with Jade when she was the only one at your court who showed any sign of caring for us...for me." It seemed the universe had tilted, and he would fall off the edge at any moment.

"It was the gesture of a child to another child. You have another duty now," Orvieto said. "Her house allowed you as a backup for her training. All your years of preparation *kata* and *tekki*, dueling skills and weapons craft, in my studio were not for your charity."

"I always worried Jade might die on a special ops mission or in the arena."

Orvieto's jaw clenched. "The game of knives can only be bested by those with a lifetime of preparation, which we have given you."

"Was it a special ops mission?"

"It's more complicated than that."

"I'll upload the scout report and go see for myself." He could not bear the thought Jade might be dead and he needed to search her out if there was any chance she might be alive.

"We forbid you to leave this world."

He forced himself to count to ten. The worst thing that ever happened to him was because he couldn't keep his mouth shut at the right time: the insult he had given to a Great House noble over a taunt about his mother. That had been Rory's first encounter with the *vendamasthra,* the "game of knives."

It wasn't Rory's fault evil men wanted his family's property, and he knew with the intellect of an adult that he had only been the catalyst, not the cause of the disaster that followed. Still, the feeling of guilt tormented him whenever he thought about it. The corner of his right eyelid twitched.

"Your tell is showing," Orvieto said.

"Screw that. Who, specifically, forbids? We'll have words later about it."

"The First Mother of Coriander bids you come to her for your orders."

This was too much. He turned to go.

"Your ship is under lock in port. If you try to leave, the paramani will impound it."

"Try and stop me."

Chapter 4: Dire News

Yanni Coriander, First Mother of Coriander, not the paramani of House Ashastra, the First Mother that ruled all humanity from the Emerald Dais, summoned Rory to the audience hall. The hall was austere compared to most houses. Only thirty meters across and a hundred meters long, teakwood parquet floor gleaming, slender white columns branching into tree-branch patterns uniting in peaked arches along the wall. The symbolic throne platform of the promised queen of legend loomed over the simple white marble nave where rested the seat of power for House Coriander incarnate. In the simple bowed wooden chair sat the woman, distant kin, known to him from childhood.

Coriander was not the most militaristic of the human houses in the galactic Commonwealth of Stars. But the First Mother of any house needed practicality to survive and Yanni had her personal bodyguard standing at her right hand. The shimmering body armor and a black and green suit with a neck scarf and thunderbolt service hashes and marked him a little lifelong servant of the house. Beauregard Morris was her paternal uncle and did not delegate her safety to anyone.

He was bald with gray-blond sideburns, a craggy brow and piercing blue eyes. He scowled. Small groups of merchants, accountants, and various functionaries of the court spoke in small groups at the periphery of the audience hall. Their eyes turned upon Rory too, as he walked in.

He paced up to Yanni and gave an obligatory knee and a curt nod and stood before her parade rest. He knew enough not to speak first, once summoned by his ruler and his second cousin. Howbeit an older one, once removed.

"Rory, pay a visit to court more often."

"Is Jade gone missing?"

She stared at him. Beauregard's gaze darkened.

"We mourn her loss with you. Jade was your playmate as a child, was she not?"

"More than that. She brought a rose from your very own garden at my father's funeral. I kept that rose and grew more."

"Once she protested her isolation from you but did her duty."

"I suppose you expect my gratitude for at least letting me see her in the sparring arena."

"No, I would have kept her away from you altogether if I could have, but someone above me had another need."

"Who? What?"

"Approach us."

Rory stammered. "But protocol?"

Beauregard tongue-lashed him and told him to hop to for once in his life.

He looked around. The functionaries and bystanders, all the court, stared.

Rory looked for the exits. Guards at every door stood impassive, faces blank. Yanni knew him too well. He had talked himself out of worse situations.

He walked onto the dais as Beauregard activated a privacy screen. They were enclosed in a bubble of random off phase continuum among the infinite possibilities of n-dimensional space. No snoop technology known to the Commonwealth of Stars, not in any of the seven sapient races, could penetrate a human tech privacy screen. Inside, the room seemed normal and light, but the oval wall enclosing them made the court look like wavering shadows underwater. The energy cost was tremendous, but within the budget of a world ruler.

He stopped, unable to contain himself, even as he regretted the cost his untimely words always incited. He barely kept the insolence out of his tone. "How is it I rate such an expensive audience, my lady?"

"The scout courier brought other news. A challenge from Sarpa."

Half of humanity feared the saurian aliens might one day ignore the Commonwealth treaty and attack humans — for sport, territory, or meat. The other half, and Rory fell into this camp, dared them to try. If he could not talk his way out of a fight, he was always one to charge into a fray if he saw no other choice.

"What concern is that to someone of my lowly estate?"

"They have done something we never expected — asked us to cede territory without a fight."

"The Consular Battlefleet will stop a war between member states. I admit I never would have thought they had the nerve just to ask for territory without a fight."

"The sarpans have laid claim to three of our colonies along the Arch Radiant."

"And we refused, of course. End of discussion."

"You know politics better than that.

He shuffled his feet, then put his hands in his pockets. "Aye, it would be a lucrative grab for them, but I doubt that the Commonwealth Council will side with them on this."

"Janjavir of House Zayan delivered the sarpan ultimatum to the paramani herself at Altarsha."

"The Zayanites are the most xenophobic house in the republic. They would feel unclean for getting within a parsec of sarpan diplomats."

Beauregard snapped. "Mind your liege's words."

Rory shook his head. "I imagine House Zayan would grovel even at your feet if it served their purpose."

"And hold a spire dagger behind her back until she got close enough to do me in."

Rory raked a hand through his hair. "They will risk losing nothing they want to a deal involving aliens."

Yanni continued. "The pirate you handed over to the colonial police had a broken star and comet tattoo from prior military service."

"Have you confirmed Jade's death?"

Yanni turned her head, not meeting his eyes.

"I thought so. I will go see for myself."

"Where will you go? Who will aid you?"

"I will learn the truth. She deserves that if she is alive, all the more if she is dead." Saying the words pierced his heart with an icicle of pain.

"What would Jade think of you if you abandoned her people to satisfy your grief?"

"Does it matter? The dead know nothing."

"But you would know. The pirate was a former Zayanite soldier, was he not?"

Much as Rory detested noble paranoia, he could not help his upbringing. Wheels within wheels. Plots within plots. Would he have killed a prisoner, he wondered, just this once? "Who can say? He might have been sent to spy on the pirates."

"To what end? The coincidental timing of Jade's death and the attack on you is too convenient."

"Even if there were a conspiracy, no one could expect us to agree to ceding any territory and sarpans can't invade without Battlefleet drawn in to stop a war between member states."

"It's a vendetta."

The Altari republic was unique among member states in permitting formal feuds under defined circumstances that would be outlawed elsewhere. The Commonwealth of Stars considered human customs a matter of their internal affairs and would not interfere as long as the feuds stayed within human territory. An open war with starships and planetary bombardment was off limits, but just about everything else was permitted.

"The Zayanites have not registered any vendettas against us lately."

"It is Sarpa that issued the challenge."

"But they think we're just low life monkeys barely out of the primordial slime."

"Think it through, cousin."

By the rules of the code duello, a vendetta could be settled by assassination "outside the city gates." But who could they target that wouldn't incite a galactic civil war? And in a territorial claim of that kind, there was no such thing as being outside republic jurisdiction. There was only one other way. "They want to settle this in a trial by combat?"

"In the grand arena on Altarsha, no less. To humiliate us and show us our place while they use our own customs to take territory."

"The Council of Stars will not let an alien race use another's customs that way."

"They have selected a champion. A sargon of their most junior creche."

"Want to rub it in, don't they?" Jade. Jade. What has become of you? He pressed his grief down into a small corner of the room in his soul where he hid his other wounds. "Jade is dead. House Coriander doesn't have a champion — they'll have to wait."

"We have ninety days to answer the challenge in the arena."

The smug smile on Beauregard's face chilled Rory's marrow. There were only a few quantum champions in known space, and they formed a clique so tight that little but rumors were known about them, all of them bad from his point of view.

"I know what you're thinking but it's suicide," Rory said.

"For an unenhanced human to fight against an eight-foot-tall saurian shod head to toe in titanium armor with claws that can rend if sword or mace doesn't get you first? Yes."

"You've got the wrong man."

"We have trained you in our court as one of our own sons for this day."

"I have never walked a mirror of the amari."

"And now you shall."

"That's what I meant about suicide."

"The *agniadarza* at the capital will test you, I'm sure you are up to it."

The Mirror of Flame was the one gifted by the amari to the human species at the beginning of the Commonwealth, to the youngest race to join. Each of the other sapient races had a mirror of their own at their capital. The mirrors were the only known technology for faster than light communication. But they had other uses, and he did not want to find out by experience what they were.

"You know I would like to whack the sarpans on their snouts any day of the week, but we have Jade to think about."

"Did I not tell you she is gone?"

"Where is the body?"

Beauregard chopped a hand to one side. "Fool boy, she was caught in a supernova blast. How could there be a body?"

Too much, he could not bear it. He clung to vain hopes. "Nothing disappears without a trace."

"We have considered all the possibilities. You will go as our emissary to Altarsha to complete our appeal for Consular intercession. If it fails, you will be where you need to be for your ordeal."

"Can't our illustrious paraman deal with it?"

"The war leader of the republic is not a quantum champion. It would be suicidal for him."

"Ashastra's champion then. Their First Sister stands for all humans. She can go."

"The Lady Chani would, but the challenge is specific to House Coriander, and by the rules of the code duello, we must answer or admit defeat and cede our colonies."

Rory shook his head. He had never met any of the rulers of the first house of the republic. Jade was gone. Maybe it was his own fault for telling her his hunch. Damn all Zayanites.

Yanni continued. "Strictly speaking, the cession would not be immediate. Judges of the change would have to be approved by the

Commonwealth Council; referendums would be held on the affected planets to determine the degree of opposition. Those wishing relocation would have to be resettled."

"Most humans would flee rather than be ruled directly by Sarpa." And what if Sarpa grew impatient? The chaos. The costs were too terrible to contemplate.

The sheen of light reflecting off Yanni's brown eyes, so like yet unlike Jade's, drew him back. "I didn't make the cut for Mahara, remember? I'm just a merchant pilot."

"The republic is held together by custom more binding than any law. We must answer the challenge or be taken as cowards and weaklings."

"Is that Zayan's game, to weaken us by any means?"

"The paramani needs you to become something more than you were."

"What do you want of me my liege?"

"Not me, the paramani Ashastra."

Beauregard spoke. "Answer her, you rogue."

Yanni touched Rory on the shoulder. "The republic has need of a champion."

Rory was ashamed to say that he felt no compassion for the world at large, but just his loss and how to make up for it. Grief and rage mixed, and he needed to act on it now, strike now.

Rory had been patient. He had played by the rules. He had been *nice*. Why hadn't he dared to make a formal bid for an arranged marriage? Asked for a quest to raise his station? Asked Jade to elope with him, persuade her to go rogue? Why?

It always came back to fear. That an ill-spoken word might hurt her, that they might set in motion the same forces that killed his father. Or was it less selfless and just cowardice?

He would mourn her loss, magnified beyond enduring if she perished because of him, and now she had. The need for vindication gave way before the dragon of vengeance. He was too small to make worlds burn for their sins. He must himself burn for them. But first he had to find out what really became of her, and he thought no words or threats would block his chosen course.

Alas, his cousin knew him. "I see you, Rory. Consider this. Can you do more to find out what became of Jade as a champion of our house, or as a rogue merchant pilot with a bounty on his head?"

The threat had the intended effect of forcing his choice, but not without raising his stubbornness to a new height. Cornered, he could not flee, and he could not fight, but he could feign surrender for his own purposes. "Alright then, when do we leave?"

"Do not betray me, Rory, or the Moon Ravens will hunt you down.
"

"You would send Battlefleet assassins after me? Are you sure that's a good idea, since you've given me a lifetime of preparation for that kind of thing?"

"Would it not be better to face one quest than a lifetime of running?"

Chapter 5: Negotiations.

Rory joined the diplomatic team for the attempted negotiation at Altarsha. Their ship, a special filtrig design teardrop configuration jump ship with extra heavy shields and armor, made port without encountering any outer planet pirates. They avoided hard targets like representatives of the ruling house. Having an escort of twelve Akasha class corvettes dispatched from the paraman's base star helped, too.

Their dropship took them directly to House Ashastra's military spaceport, landing tail down to the floating docks in Urbmar harbor. The oldest city of the republic sprawled on the twin arms of the mountain ranges that joined further north into the spine of mountains that divided Altarsha's sole continent in half.

A skimmer took them over the crashing blue waves under Altarsha's harsh white sun. Ichthyosaur fins broke the surf a bare kilometer away, and he hoped the ultra-sonar's field was operating at full efficiency to keep a leviathan from making a snack of them. The ride exhilarated him, but the audience to come cowed him as nothing else had before.

Rory's party checked in through the Eagle's gate. House guards in white and green Ashastra uniforms escorted them to the diplomatic quarter, where aliens kept all their ambassadors and the human houses had their own manors.

The Grand Arena where the powerful wanted him to fight was north, in the shadow of the Shield mountains.

They left him to stew in an apartment for a night and a day, twiddling his thumbs and snacking on petite fours and tea. He wanted black coffee and lots of it. Damn the diplomatic customs. Besides which, he didn't like being treated like a peon, not that it wasn't a luxurious cage.

A peremptory knock on his door announced his summons.

The Altari republic eschewed titles like emperor or empress, but the First Mother of all humans, the paramani, "highest of the first" in the old tongue, might as well be one. He wondered with all the pomp and circumstance why they didn't just call her a queen and be done with it. Yet no one had ever explained why Altari nobles hated the title. Mere suggestions of such could trigger a coup. The people in the street didn't feel the same way. Folklore pronounced that the Queen would bring the freedom they yearned for.

His escort, a blank faced guard in the white and gold uniform of the Ashastra personal guard led him along a corridor tiled in white and green, the ceiling ornate floral intaglio of an exotic wood with a spiral grain pattern — and spy eyes studded throughout. He could just imagine the hidden armaments in what felt like a killing zone to him.

The hall ended at an elevator; the entrance bracketed by plain suited men in green suits and mirrored face HUDs standing stock still with their hands folded in front of them.

"Where are you taking me?" he asked the guard.

"Up, my lord," he answered, spine stiff with protocol and unsmiling. He placed his palm in front of the golden panel on the side of the door. A moire pattern fluoresced, a green bar with a white indicator mark one third of the way up. At the top of the bar the stooping delta and eagle wing emblem of House Ashashtra, at the bottom a skull and crossbones icon.

"What's down, I wonder," he spoke, looking nowhere in particular and trying to act as nonchalant as possible.

"The dungeon, sir."

"And up?"

The guard sighed. "A moment, my lord. Give it a moment."

It felt like his heart might drop out of his chest as the elevator accelerated upwards, noiseless. Too bad no one had ever invented teleportation pads. He had heard tall tales in bars about amari being able to teleport, but he had found no official information on the subject.

The door whisked open as the elevator eased to a stop. The doors opened to a bright cloudless blue sky and a searing white light. He stepped out. Before him, there was spread a wide pavilion with peaked white canopies and green pennants flapping in the wind.

A seneschal of the household guard, a woman about his age, in ceremonial chain mail and surplice greeted him. "I am Suraneem, Seneschal to the paramani Loyola Ashastra." She had short cropped blonde hair, ice-blue eyes, and would have enticed him to approach under other circumstances. His face heated.

She blushed and cleared her throat.

"This way, my lord."

Shadows beat the pavement in front of him. Turning he saw the twelve flagpoles arrayed in an arc behind the lift he had arrived in. All the twelve flags of mankind's great houses. Coriander's waved with them and he reminded himself that he was kin and had done nothing to deserve the paramani's wrath. He straightened and lifted his chin.

He followed Suraneem, a slow promenade up a blue carpet bracketed by raised floral beds and cherry trees, the blossoms of spring turning to summer.

The center of the rooftop plaza held the *Mara* pavilion. The Altari word translated into Galactic as "Peace." But a slight addition and it became the word for war. Rory, having grown up in a house that favored art and poetry, was not lost on the subtlety. He wondered how this day would end.

The rooftop spanned hectares, and the pavilion could hold a troop of dignitaries and their bodyguards and attendants. A pair of curtain walls of the pavilion had been rolled up to allow the sea breeze from Urbmar harbor to gust through.

This high, he supposed snoops could be warded. At the front of the arched way, two holo columns radiated upwards like memorial columns inscribed in shimmering colors with the winged delta sigil of House Ashastra on his right. On his left, the glittering column was black superimposed by intertwining helixes in seven colors representing the seven sapient species of known space.

The pavilion inside was arranged with two concentric circles of tables with one end open to a low dais with the paramani's seat, not the formal one on the throne room in the palace proper, but it marked her place. It was empty for the moment.

He made his way to the House Coriander section. There were about thirty attendants altogether, divided up among the various camps, one for Sarpa, one for his house, and a handful of observers from other houses. He spied the broken star and comet banner of House Zayan, orange and black, among them, and tried not to stare. House Selene was also present under their silver moon banner.

Several of the scribes were aliens. He saw a tall saren with his bloodhound jowls and spatulate fingers standing arms crossed looking skeptical while a harirossa, bipedal with a sea lion like face and dog ears lectured him. She was dressed in a blue robe and feathered beret, poet's livery, and her barky voice broke into a truncated yodel as she tried to convince her counterpart of whatever it was. It was well known you could hardly get a word out of sarens and seldom could stop a harirossa from drowning you in them.

Beauregard jostled him. "About time."

The accusing tone forced a response. Rory sniffed. "I am exactly where the paramani wants me to be in the exact moment she wants me to be here as are you, Uncle."

"Look at those sarpan miscreants."

The sarpan delegation was composed of the subspecies biological castes as usual. The five-foot-high soldier caste, the raptors, milled about their masters — a trio of sargon caste sarpans between eight and ten feet tall. The largest was a sargon female.

The raptors were sapient, after a fashion, with just enough IQ to follow orders. They wore vests and half breeches; their dew claws rapped on the tile floor as they skittered about, bobbing and waving their necks, looking for the next drink or food, baring their rows of serrated teeth in their narrow long jaws, their grins a caricature of a human smile.

The sargons, Rory understood, had the same intelligence range as smarter humans, and were just as aggressive and almost as cagey. No overlords were here; they towered over sargons and rarely left their home creches.

Two of the sargons wore robes, one black, one green. They were functionaries, though they could have tried to hide weapons under those voluminous folds and the black hoods hanging loose around their craggy scaled heads.

The tall one wore a blood red tunic and kilt with the triple lightning and serpent badge representing the Sarpan Empire and a gold scroll on the opposite collar representing the diplomatic corps. She introduced herself as Arkasa. Her galactic grammar was book perfect, her accent difficult to follow without a spectrum filter earphone.

Seneschal Suranameen called the meeting to order on behalf of the paramani, though the paramani herself was not yet present. Arkasa presented the facts as she saw them.

As ambassador to the humans, she could stand for the Council as Sarpa's representative, giving him cause for worry. Part of Rory's martial arts training was in reading tells of aliens. Arkasa's lips curled at their corners as she spoke, baring her molar fangs, evidence of her displeasure.

"House Snatha, the greens, insist on pressing their claim to the Aldebaran colonies, dubbed the Arch Radiant by the Altari Republic. House Sargosan, the blacks who serve the overlord are indifferent to their claim but not opposed.

"It would be expedient for the humans to cede the disputed worlds as exchange for a bounty payment in lieu of war."

The saren raised his hand.

"The chair recognizes Ambassador Volk."

"By what circuitous serpent logic doses Sarpa claim right to another species' worlds?"

Arkasa's tongue flicked in and out. "What part of the word 'empire' do you not understand?" She wheezed out a chuckle. "I direct your attention to Convention 624 of the Commonwealth of Stars charter..."

The essence of Arkasa's point was that humans were known for their indefatigable quarrelsomeness and had devised the code duello to mitigate the risk of war. The Arch Radiant colonies were too close to the sarpan border for the empire's comfort. The placement of house guard militaries that came and went, hiding under the banner of internal affairs, while the consular navy left them alone to oppress sarpan residents was intolerable. Since humans had refused to cede without a fight, they would get one under their own code.

"I am informed by a House Zayan representative that the expected Coriander champion perished in an unfortunate stellar mishap. House Coriander must supply a replacement within 90 days of this meeting, or they default by their own rules. As representative of the council, I assure you, Sarpa will follow your law assiduously."

Beauregard elbowed Rory. "Come on then, you're up."

Rory shook him off. Whispering. "Up for what? They're still negotiating."

"Excuse me." The harirossa delegate interrupted them.

"Shoo," Beauregard told her. "I'm prodding my nephew to do the right thing."

"Obviously. My name is Dwendamarminomimossa." She cleared her throat. "I know that is much for your limited vocal abilities. You may call me Min."

"I don't want to call you anything," Beauregard snapped. "Be off."

"I do not blame the young master for his fear; it would be right for him to flee and save his life from a sargon warrior. Quite right."

Rory bristled. "Who asked you?"

"May I have your comm address so I can compose a poem relating your cowardice, or a lay about your heroic death should you muster enough courage to die like a man?"

This was too much for Rory. He pointed an index finger at Min and held it there, his mouth working without any words coming out. Then he turned and walked out of the meeting.

Two of the green suited paramani's guards met him. Their HUD mirror stares compelled Rory to halt.

"Why my leash? The paramani has plenty of closer relatives with more experience to do diplomacy."

"Wait with us, my lord."

"And this 'lord' business. I am so far down the inheritance ladder, none of you should care about me more than an accountant." He knew the argument was lame. Orvieto's admission of his real purpose left little doubt that he was just a widget, a spare part, a contingency, Plan B when plan A had failed. "So, I'll just leave, no?"

They bracketed him as he reentered. The oral arguments had ceased, and delegates were streaming in the other direction out. Beauregard passed him and winked. Only Arkasa remained, all eight feet of her. He folded his arms and looked at her.

"I do not blame or praise you Rory Demaris ni Coriander," Arkasa said. "We have both been dragged into this folly by conspirators on both sides."

"I protest. I renounced court politics to be a merchant."

"You cannot escape your blood or your training. Do you refuse?" Her tongue flicked out, a sign she thought to win, that he would renege on his duty.

Still, he could not help but bluster. "You are the diplomat to mankind. How is your problem my business? For that matter how is a sarpan diplomat not a contradiction in terms?"

"Will you consent to your sovereign's wishes to fight our champion?"

"Suicide is not an option."

"Then choose victory."

"How?"

"I do not know a human's path out of a fox trap, but your reputation suggests you will find a way. You have twenty-four hours to answer, three months to prepare if you accept the challenge."

There were too many forces closing in on him to dodge them all. Then he would deal with one problem at a time. "I accept."

Her tongue flicked out in surprise. "So quickly do you choose death."

"I have enough experience with you sarpans and republic politics to know when I'm cornered. Remember. I have three months to figure out the rest."

"Perhaps a fool, perhaps a hero. I salute you." With that, she bowed her head and departed.

After the ambassador left, a slow clapping sounded from the curtains behind the paramani's seat. A slender woman, white-haired with a sleeveless green ankle length dress embroidered with a swirl of white stars up to her shoulders. She wore a silver circlet.

"You were watching all along?"

"It behooves a ruler to observe sometimes and choose her moment of entrance.

"The Sarpan Empire wants the Aldebaran colonies for their own." They were some of the lushest, most profitable planets in the republic, or Commonwealth, for that matter.

"And what would you like me to do about it, Auntie?"

"You know the *Gita'Adarza*?

Rory's ancient Altari was rusty, not the least because the classical language was proscribed for common use. No one had ever told him why, but everyone knew the title rendered from the Altari into Common Galactic as *The Saga of the Mirrors*.

"The mirrors of the amari are more than glorified faster-than-light radio."

"So, I have guessed by the body count recorded in the annals."

"Mostly of interlopers who trespassed on them. Those who are sent by proper authority fare better."

"Better? If you regard yourself as fortunate for only falling a hundred feet without a parachute instead of a thousand."

"Yet some have survived the hundred-foot drop. You are not a quantum champion yet. Most of your training is complete, or you would have no time for your last step of preparation."

Rory pinched his forehead with his right hand and shut his eyes tight. "Prepare me all you want, but if I find a better way out of this trap, I will take it."

"Is it better to face the bully that wants to take what's yours or would you rather run? My sister told me you were our best chance to turn Sarpa back on its heels. Was she wrong?"

"How would she know? I have never met her."

"I am the paramani and you will go to the mirror with my mandate. The First Sister will brief you."

Chapter 6: A Familiar Stranger

Afterwards, on the way to his temporary quarters in the palace, something bothered Rory about the synchronicity between Jade's death and the pirate attack on him.

A palace guardsman took him to the personal living residences of the Ashastra matrilineal family.

His quarters followed Coriander tastes, subdued lighting, wooden panels and woven mats, with hanging vines and trickle fountains at every hallway. The meditation room had a low table with parchment and archival paper, along with ink pots and brushes.

Jade taught him the brush techniques for watercolors and poetry. The tradition was older than the republic and while most houses had left it behind for speed and glittering technology, he found it soothing.

Still troubled by a nagging sense of ignorance, he commed Joort on a secure link and asked him about the coincidence of the attacks on him and Jade.

There was a prolonged silence before Joort answered. "What is so unusual about conspiracy among nobles?"

"You think the *vendamasthra* is behind this, but which house, and why?"

"Who is Coriander's worst enemy?"

Rory could not give an answer. A knock on the door summoned him and he told Joort to watch his back. The seneschal had arrived to direct him to his transport.

The base star for the home fleet, orbiting Altarsha, loomed as the transport approached. It was a tapered cylinder with stepped sides that looked much like the gargantuan version of the top Rory spun to amuse himself when bored. Only this "top" housed 10,000 full-time house guard military and attached Battlefleet personnel. Hundreds of missile hard points, rotary lasers, rail guns and likely weapons unknown to

Rory made up the armaments complement of the base star which could obliterate anything but a full-blown war fleet threatening Altarsha.

He felt out of place in the space dock waiting area. He tried to make his merchant cargo pants relatively well pressed and his leather flight jacket with the sheep's wool collar was at its best. The dark brown, almost black Veldebeest hide buffed to a commercial shine if not spit and polished military perfection.

Lady Chani arrived in a trident fighter which docked on suspensor fields at the edge of the landing bay as the bay star shut its armored hatches behind it. Three separate pilots climbed out of their cockpit bubbles. Two human ones and a taller lankier one that must have been a sarin according to Rory's reckoning. All of them wore black flight suits with Battlefleet unit markers and insignia. Their helmets were opaque, and the trio walked up into the landing bay. The center figure, a woman, paused and nodded to each of the other two figures. One of the two figures beside her was a saren who unmasked its faceplate revealing the dark soulful eyes bloodhound nodded to her and left. The other pilot, a human who wore command pilot wings, likewise opened his faceplate, saluted and with a crisp quarter turn strode past Rory ignoring him. The woman undid her helmet and tucked it under one arm. She was slight of build with an elfin face and black hair with wisps of gray and just the beginnings of wrinkles under her eyes. Rory bowed his head to greet her.

A cheerful voice said, "So, Rory Demaris ni Coriander, how goes your battle with yourself?"

That voice.

"Don't look so stunned, Rory, I have known you since you were eight years old."

The voice remembered so well had aged only a little, a woman's voice barely of age when she first taught him his martial arts forms. He never knew she was a Battlefleet starship pilot. He had no rank to deserve such a master and assumed Jade had extended yet another kindness to him after the duel. Unless....

With alacrity he bowed, concealing his confusion, nodding. He remembered her too well as the mysterious woman given to him as his first martial arts teacher after his father died and his family fell from grace. One of the few kind strangers in the chaos that had engulfed him, no one had ever explained who she was. He knew her only as *sensei*, "master", before she had disappeared one day as soon as she had appeared, and left him to Orvieto as his trainer ever after. "I never knew your name..."

"It is a shock I know. I treasured those two years on Coriander. I rue that I could not make a better goodbye at the time. Know that I mourn with you."

He cast his eyes down.

"You wonder how I am a starship pilot with Battlefleet. That is the least of my duties."

It dawned on him that her House shield was for Ashastra, and she had a command star for a permanent field command. She left when he reached his first degree black belt. He was only seventeen. His mother had died of grief two years earlier, and he had felt orphaned a second time. "I wondered why you had left us and who you might have been assigned to instruct after Jade and me."

"The paraman perhaps?"

"It would be fitting training for the consul to the Commonwealth."

"Fitting, but he had no need of instruction from me, for we learned from the same master from when we could first walk."

"Rory. Recollect yourself. I must report to my brother, Narya."

"The paraman?"

"Peace is an illusion. There is always a war somewhere and so I report to our war leader."

"*You* are the Lady Chani?" The second most powerful human in known space, and she had been his teacher. What game was he caught up in? How far did it go back? He felt as if an abyss had opened before his feet.

"I am. Let us speak to your need. Join me." With that she motioned down the corridor. He could not resist staring at her shoulder patch. It read the insignia of the Battlestar Fury of Aldebaran. She caught him looking at her shoulder patch. "Yes, name from the home world of the arch radiant. Presently under your house's dominion. We will speak of this later"

She dismissed him to his quarters.

An adjutant came later, a tall willowy woman wearing Battlefleet service dress and the Jaguar Bow sword shoulder patch. Only graduates of the galactic academy at Mahara wore such badges. He chided himself for the pang of envy that passed like a wave through him.

She bade him wear the house guard uniform provided, with the sign of Coriander and his merchant guild service ribbons. Unused to the formality but knowing better than to refuse, he complied. The adjutant escorted him to the presidential level of the base star, just below the flag command level. He passed through the paraman's wardroom to a formal dining room set in full splendor of gold filigreed crystal and silver settings.

The paraman, who looked as youthful as Rory except for his shock of white hair wore the midnight blue and silver service dress uniform of the Consular Battlefleet. He had many more ribbons than Rory could earn in a lifetime, and two command insignia, one as war leader of the republic and the other as Consul to the Commonwealth of Stars where he represented the interests of humanity at the behest of the twelve first mothers of human space.

Jade was beautiful in a way that could never be reproduced, but Chani would have dominated a ballroom of nobles in her current regalia. She wore a white gown with a blue and white cloak clasped crosswise to her left shoulder. The brooch, all of diamonds and emeralds could have been a down payment on a new starship and shaped with the canted green delta and white wings like a stooping bird of prey, the house sigil of Ashastra.

Her eyes followed his to her brooch. "Yes, Rory, I am first among sisters in our house."

Not until today had he ever suspected his sensei to be second in line to rule human space. The champion of House Ashastra shunned the spotlight, and he had never seen a picture of her. Lady Chani. First Sister not of just of her own House but of all the Houses of the republic.

"My lady," he choked out the words.

"I am still your sensei, now sit and have some tea before the main course."

He looked up. She was smiling at him and extended a hand. He took it feeling embarrassed. She had a firm grip and led him to his seat to her right and just two down from the paraman at one end. The senior officers, men and women of Battlefleet, eyes stared as if to wonder why an interloper had won pride of place. At the other end of the table was the empty chair reserved for the paramani when she chose to leave the steady earth.

"Don't look so abashed, Rory. I have great admiration for brave souls in your position."

"I wouldn't credit me too early, Mistress."

She arched an eyebrow. "I hear from your friend, Mr. Joort that you are partial to filtrig liquor? You must settle for tea for now."

"As you wish."

They ate in silence with a meal that was previously prepared by the stewards at a fixed menu. By the time they got to the end they've had the customary small talk. She had asked about the paramani's health and he had made the obligatory answers, generic, if truthful. He reciprocated asking about health of the Paramani of Altarsha and court life and which team she thought would win in the next set of football matches. He shied away from asking about the grand arena.

At the end the stewards brought them coffee. The paraman had not said more than casual court wishes for his health though he did inquire of Rory's ship the Cormorant, and for a span of minutes they had a pleasant discussion on ship design.

"May I ask the purpose of inviting me to dinner, your graces?"

The paraman poured a glass of wine. The scent was a good vintage and the light from the crystal chandelier gleamed flickering flame on the goblet. "Much can be told of the measure of a man over dinner."

"Even by sight it is difficult to judge a man, and no woman should be rebuked without seeing for yourself if she deserves it."

"Do you rebuke me now, Demaris?"

"I only point out our common obligations to decency."

Chani interrupted them. "Enough male jousting."

Rory felt chagrined, the paraman puffed air out of his cheeks.

The paraman changed the subject. "Your sensei tells me you are an even better student than Jade when you were learning your combat forms."

"Yes, that's me. Always ready, never chosen." The words, bitter, came out faster than he could restrain himself. *Jade, why didn't you choose me before it was too late?*

A look of sympathy crossed Chani's eyes. "You must put behind your loss."

"I'm not convinced Jade is really gone. Do we not have a proverb that nothing disappears without a trace?"

"Set your grief aside for your people, *Jade's* people

Rory felt his only way to be sure about Jade's fate would be to tread the same path she had gone wherever it led. "I don't know what I feel anymore. What must I do?"

"Do you know what makes a champion besides martial arts training and a ready heart?"

"No mistress."

"You must pass an ordeal with a mirror of the amari."

Rory poured himself a glass of golden wine. "So, the paramani said. I feel you have invited me to a last meal for a condemned man. What more can I say?"

The paraman interrupted. "Do not change the subject. Your ship travels far and frequently. Jade told us you suspected a possible cause of the unusual shifting of in space jump lanes."

Rory squirmed. Under a ruler's microscope he did not want to be. But what to give away and what to conceal? A misspoken word could lead to misfortune or death. *Put no trust in princes.*

The paraman rapped his fingers on the table. "Well?"

"I think this is excellent wine, my lord paraman. Yes."

"Yes?"

"Yes."

"Could you elaborate more? Tell me your theory."

"I cannot, my Lord."

"And why not?"

"I am constrained by lack of data since I have been forced to this table by circumstance and politics." *Mothers, what has my tongue gotten me into now?*

Chani drew in a breath and held it, studying them both. The paraman shook his head, a trace of a smile. She breathed again.

"If you survive to be champion, I will enjoy seeing the other Great Houses humbled by your ascent."

"What is that to me?" *Jade, are you truly dead?*

The paraman studied him. Rory felt like he was being judged and found wanting.

The paraman continued. "Whatever customs we maintain in the code duello to prevent war, if strained too far, the failsafe will break. I will not risk you getting anywhere near the *agniadarza* until I am satisfied you will not draw the wrath of the amari down on us."

Rory wondered what the wrath might be about. He was tired of always hearing about the mighty amari and their precious gifts to primitive sapients. "My lord, I have never seen an amari. Are you sure there are any left to pester us?"

The paraman shook his head and frowned. "Chani, do something with him. I will defer to your word as our house champion."

Chani dabbed her lips with a napkin and set it down, arranging a knife on it with exactitude. "Three days from now we would have gone to the mirror of flame. But first, I will see the measure of you for myself before I risk three planets' fate on someone who will not share what he knows nor knows when to be silent."

Chapter 7: Secret Wounds

She visited him in his stateroom later, accompanied by two space marines with carbines. Was he to be arrested? He stood and bowed, in the fashion of his home world.

"I wish for all we knew of each other growing up that you would look past rank and your wounds and trust me as your sensei."

"What do you know of my wounds, my lady?"

"Enough. Jade spoke of you often over the years I was on Coriander. She loved you, you know."

His eyes drifted to a corner of the ceiling.

"So? You doubt yourself in even that?"

He clenched his fists at his side.

"Report to the flight deck in one hour. The suit rigger will equip you for your ride."

"Where are we going?"

"Mahara."

"But that's a three-week jump in a hauler."

"Surely."

"It's suicidal enough for me to try to be your champion in the time left. Can we afford three weeks?"

"We cannot afford to be wrong about you. Since you will not tell us what you know we will jump in a Battlefleet deep space raider down enough bands for my purpose."

"How many bands?"

"Four, maybe more," she said.

"Four. That must be a hell of a ship. How many more?"

"If we run into an anomaly, I will make you deal with it."

"You flatter me."

"You know better than that, student."

"Yes, sensei."

The only planet whose location was guarded more, was Priamar, and no one knew, officially, the coordinates for the amari home world. As it was, the trip rushed past in the fury of a deep space dive. The ship, unnamed except for an experimental designator XS for shrike class, a needle tipped delta configuration, with enough space for three crew. There were racks to sleep in against the bulkhead.

Rory felt nauseated after the tidal forces, uncompensated fully, played with his guts the whole time. He shivered on reentry into normal space. The cockpit had a paired pilot configuration, so sitting next to Chani, could not conceal his discomfort as he grimaced. They could see each other's face on their respective helmet HUDs.

"You have raced before I heard?" Chani's voice came in over the comm.

"Aye. No racer I ever piloted could go six bands down. How much more can she do?"

"We are not certain. A human piloted ship is limited by our grav compensation tech."

Rory reviewed the engine telemetry. "She's a work of art. Looks like you have filtrig hands all over the design, and goyas too judging from the sensor suite."

"Ashastra shipyards has many resources. Brace yourself."

A Battlefleet flotilla with ships contributed from every major alien species in the commonwealth held the permanent garrison to protect Mahara. The largest, a dreadnought class monitor a spheroid bristling with laser and missile batteries made a formidable guard.

"You could pulverize any raiders with that force."

"That is what you see. The amari insist on their own defense posture to guarantee the peace, and the lives of the students here."

"Are their defenses as invisible as they are, sensei?" The banter reminded him of better days when Jade and he had been her students, and the world seemed less complicated.

"You speak more truly than you know."

The Shrike bypassed the spaceport on an elliptical orbit burn sighting on a spatial anomaly of the known kind, Mahara's secondary suns being sucked into an invisible whirlpool, a black hole.

"My lady, there was no natural way for that thing to be so near a habitable system. Did the amari construct it as a power source?"

The ship bucked as the gravity waves from the distortion tripped fail-safes in the drive which Chani immediately overrode.

"Show me your plot for a whipsaw maneuver."

He hesitated.

"There is little time for evading my wishes."

"You already know I'm a good pilot." In fact, he was one of the best and stalled as long as he could. There were at least a couple of minutes to pull back.

The shuddering intensified. Chani's voice grated. "This is childish. Do the maneuver."

Rory wondered how willing she was to chance death. He wasn't ready to give up on Jade, though. His hands flew over the console as he took the helm and executed a perfect maneuver. They pressed back into their seats and a weight like an anvil pushed him slowly to the right, the wraparound buffer of the seat holding him in, the automatic straps tightened. He grunted.

The maneuver ran its course. He exhaled. The black hole trailed them. Grumbling under his breath, he released the helm as the shrike coasted.

Chani plotted another vector in, faster and steeper. "Now do it again."

She had him repeat a thousand-kilometer intervals. He swallowed hard, acid rising in his throat, The changes in warping of local space didn't match the distance and gravitational surge. "The instruments are distorting, are you sure this is a good idea?"

The ship shuddered, the nose yawed sixty degrees, then came back true under the pilot's adjustment.

"I knew this wasn't a good idea," he said.

"Run the plot."

"No! The instrument calibration is distorted."

"This singularity has been mapped to exhausting detail. Follow the instruments."

If he followed the instruments, they would die. If he took over on instinct, she would know his secret. Damn. Damn. Damn.

"You do it if you're so sure."

Chani muttered an invective. She took the helm. The ship vibrated, sluggish. She frowned.

He would give her bare enough time to see if he could keep his secret.

The engines screamed as they spooled up fighting the gravity wave.

Watching Chani struggle as his intuition felt the surges of n-space, with a sinking heart he realized what must have happened to Jade. Their common enemy had an instrument that could warp interdimensional gravity waves, with Jade its first victim. He felt for the first time that she might really be dead. Be lost to him forever.

"Aw, felgercarb," he said. "I have the helm."

Riding on instinct, he adjusted the velocity vector by a tenth of a degree, then another tenth. After another series of adjustments, the ship shot around the singularity at fractional light speed. Fortunately the inertial compensator didn't burn out or they would have been pasted across the canopy.

Chani did not speak for several minutes. "Why do you take chances with your life like that? With *my* life."

"You drag me into your vendettas; you risk the consequences."

"Do not mock me Rory, I knew you when your were a youth and without guile. How did you know the instruments were off?"

"I just did. Some other n-space distortion must be acting to warp the gravity gradients."

"Induced? How?"

"Jade believed me." His voice flat. He felt exposed out here. Anyone high in republic politics could be an enemy.

"Tell me." The nose yawed forty degrees right. The helm shuddered as Chani recovered control.

"What kind of game is this First Sister?"

"What could do this to our ship from a stationary black hole?"

"A pulsar. But why would a pulsar only be readable on close approach?"

She veered off. "Answer me that riddle and when we make it back to Altarsha, I will tell you."

He wondered if he should tell her about the Zayanite mercenary. It might draw her suspicions away from him. "I had no idea becoming a champion was this byzantine."

"We do not know fully the amari's motives for letting you approach a mirror. I must be sure of your loyalty to let you anywhere near the Mirror of Flame."

That tore it. "Fine. When we get back. If some Zayanite scum doesn't bushwhack me a second time, I'll tell you." Oops.

She made him tell her the rest of the story on the pirate raid on the way back, and amazingly no humans attacked them. Nor aliens. But a drone followed their wake halfway back and transmitted a distress call. From Coriander. "The sarpans made an unannounced diplomatic visit to your home world. Chani answered. Paramani Coriander has appealed for a Commonwealth observer. They won't be satisfied with an alien Consul."

"So, you have to go there?"

"No."

"Uh. You're the only one of Consular rank on board unless of those invisible amari are here."

"Stop saying they're invisible. They rarely do that, the energy costs are too high."

"Well that's even more reassuring."

"We are going forthwith to the Mirror of Flame."

"I thought you had to decide if you could trust me."

"Do you understand what the spatial anomaly is now?"

"It has to be a beacon. A pulsar used like a lighthouse, warning ships off the shoals."

"Then why only broadcast when you are dangerously close?"

"What if someone tampered with it?. But I think someone has a weapon that can affect similar gravity concentrations." No one knew how old the amari were or who their enemies might have been.

"Probabilities are shifting in unexpected ways. We must add your talent to the champions to shift the balance back towards order.

"And what if I refuse to continue?"

"The alternative is chaos."

"So now you trust me?"

"All except your wound about your father, but I have no choice now. The risk is acceptable."

"Why?"

"Anyone the sarpans fear enough to intimidate a world ruler and risk Council retribution is worth turning into a weapon against our enemies."

"Is that all I am now, sensei, a weapon?"

"Not yet."

She let him rest for three days at the palace then took him to the Mirror of Flame.

Chapter 8: The Mirror of Flame

Chani accompanied Rory to the Mirror of Flame for his introduction. He knew that the Mirror of Flame was located somewhere on the palace grounds. The artifact was ancient, a gift to the Amari back when humans were still relatively primitive. Before even the invention of steam power.

"Are we going to the palace?" asked Rory. He wore the gray and black fatigues of a house guard military without insignia. He missed his merchanter gear. Still, he was excited about the prospect of seeing the emerald dais for the first time.

"What makes you think we're going to the palace?" asked Chani.

"Well, for one thing we're headed in that general direction."

The palace itself was much older than most of the rest of the compound. It had the appearance of a square stone structure with a central dome without a capital. There were no columns making up the walls. They were etched in thousands of rows of abstract symbols, thought to be a lost script of their forbearers. Rory recognized this as much because he was from House Coriander where they held an annual symposium for poets from all regions of the commonwealth and he had heard a Hari Rossa scholar comment on the puzzle of the palace script.

"I was just hoping to see the reception hall."

"You just want to see the emerald dais."

He blushed. "True, it is not the same as pictures. Perhaps at the next jubilee."

"But that's seven years away."

"Well, let's hope you survive until then," she said.

Rory knew that audiences at the center of human power in the galaxy were rare. Not for the first time did he chafe at being so low within the ranks of the nobility. A simple accounting steward would have a better chance of seeing the emerald dais than him. He wondered if in his excitement or apprehension at their previous meeting he had totally missed the location of the *agniadarza*, the Mirror of Flame.

Chani herself or the full noble regalia of House Ashastra complete with green gown, white cape, emerald broach and the command star also in the form of a brooch over her right breast marking her as the first sister and champion of Altarsha. The gown had half-sleeves, and he saw a glimmer of color, a pattern on her skin inside her forearm that looked like curls of frozen smoke.

They came to the same elevator that had taken him to the rooftop. The plainclothes guards in the green suits averted their eyes this time when Chani approached taking care to salute before doing so as if saying 'your business is too secret for my regard'. They entered the elevator. A prickle of anxiety tickled the back of Rory's neck. Chani spoke a word. The elevator descended rapidly. The lights marched down towards the skull and crossbones.

"The mirror is in the dungeon?"

She shook her head. "Wait and see."

When they reached the skull and crossbones level, the light passed one beyond at the bottom of the plate in the moire pattern appeared, gray, white and blue radiating in an illusion of motion. Or was it an illusion? The motion eased, and the doors slid open. Flanking this doorway were two guards in strange apparel. They were likewise robed from head to toe with black and black with red cowls and held energy pikes at attention. They were motionless. The front of their circles had a red shield with a black swan on them. Rory had heard of the "swords" at the Battlefleet Academy at Mahara but had never actually seen anyone wearing signs of that regalia. There were 12 swords representing different disciplines within the Academy to which any alien race might become a member. It was a way of binding together the different species of the commonwealth of stars into one military. It also introduced factionalism and service rivalry. The corridor was long, made up of a gold and white tiled floor. A rectangular hallway that seemed to lead to infinity. Spy eyes were dotted on the ceiling and Rory spotted blisters along the wall that must be security lasers.

"Well, the security is impressive. I wonder what else they've added to this? Poison gas maybe?"

Chani murmured, "Perhaps."

They next entered an atrium to continue the impression in Rory's mind of an ancient temple.

He wondered how many years had passed for the ground-level to be so much higher. "When was this built?"

"An age ago," Chani said. "Be silent now as we enter the operations room."

The doors opened silently and as they walked into a huge, dimly lit chamber. The scene became more familiar to him. He reminded him of the bridge of the capital class battle fleet dreadnought. However, in this case instead of a central holographic disc with the bridge arrayed around it, the disc seemed to take up the entire chamber which must have been at least 30 m across. This was the mirror-flame room, and all Rory could see was a black disc. It took something like inert basalt or carbon fiber. There were no projection ports around the railing and metal lattice work enclosing the structure. The encircling metal looked like stainless steel with a bronze tint to it. Tendrils of light meandered across the struts. They exited onto a platform large enough for a small company of starship troopers at one end of the mirror, and the mirror operator sat at a console with multiple virtual monitor screens that lit up her face like a ghost. She wore a standard battle fleet officer midnight blue and silver service dress uniform, and her shoulder patch marked her as a member of the Black Swan sword, the operators of special weapons and technology in the Commonwealth of Stars.

"Excuse me, my lady..." he asked Chani in a whisper.

"Shhh..."

The operator completed whatever task she was logging. The chamber was almost entirely silent condition were over a ventilation fan whispered into the gallery. The air smelled fresh but with a tang unfamiliar to Rory. Perhaps cinnamon? The ceiling over them was vaulted, but the arches seemed indistinct to his eyes as if he were suddenly nearsighted and could not quite make out the lines.

"My head feels odd," he said.

Chani shivered. "It is not often that one is sent into the mirror itself. You should survive, since you go under orders and it respects authority congruent with its programming."

"*Should* survive? I thought this was just an introduction."

Chani placed a hand on the identification plate. Her hand backlit from the plate showing in her fingers glowed red in the light. She spoke words ancient with authority. His rank and the Coriander world's fascination with culture and history provided a rudimentary understanding. The law forbade lower castes to learn it, and to speak it openly carried the risk of proscription. *Legend has it that ancient Altari was the language first spoken by humans at the time of their awakening.* The air pressure seemed to press down upon Rory like the weight of millennia. His heart pounded. He found it hard to breathe. Horror crept at the edges of his mind.

The console operator averted her eyes as Chani spoke, and the virtual display monitor switched to a golden lines flowing in a bar and curled script, mostly unintelligible to Rory. One word stood out, *mortar,* "death."

A voice, like a cascading waterfall, came from the speaker. *Sacate anavirita vaniksaksikam,* it said.

"What does that mean?" he said.

"Seek the way that was lost," Chani answered.

"What way? And what does it have to do with death?"

She studied him. "Who taught you this?"

"I only know a few words from a *harirossa* tutor on Coriander."

"As I said." Chani dismissed the mirror operator who bowed and left, the doors sliding shut with a whisper in the tomb like air. She motioned him to sit in the operator's chair. "The mirror has granted you an audience."

Rory refused to be moved. "You have no right to force alien contact on me."

"I have had enough of your provincial narcissism."

"As opposed to imperial coercion?"

Her face smoothed with the stare of a martial arts master wiping out all tells before a fatal strike. "You are free to leave. The paraman doubts you. I thought you better than a coward."

"And the consequence?" buying time to think.

Her right arm extended, he saw a flickering light on her forearm, even as her hand pushed him towards the chair. "Sit. You do not have a neural implant to hear the mirror, and the next words are for your ears only." She set operator headphones on him. "Listen and watch. I will leave and return in one hour."

"I don't understand. How would you know how long it will take?"

"The mirrors of the amari are connected not only to each other, but to every point in space-time across all the continuums of n-dimensional space. Time flows differently when communing with a mirror. Even if it invites you in, no one is ever gone for more than an hour."

"Never?"

"If you walk a mirror of eternity and do not return in an hour, you never will."

"What if I refuse?"

"Of course you can choose disgrace instead of duty."

Rory pondered the possibility of death. A mad thought entered his mind that if he died, he might be reunited with Jade. But the Altari do not believe in gods or the afterlife. They have made themselves their own gods. It was easier for humans when they were primitives and worshiped Sarpa as their god. But death is a journey in one direction, and except for a human legend from their most ancient days' there has never been a hint that anyone might be an exception. Rory did not really want to die, not just yet. But to live branded as a coward?

Chani took his silence for agreement. "The mirror is strict about its protocols. Be well Rory Demaris ni Coriander" She turned her back and left. As the door fell shut, Rory was now as alone as he felt.

The console lit up with letters and standard galactic words in common script. The headphones crackled with static or was that the sound of flames consuming a forest?

The mirror sent a single cryptic message. "Are you willing from your heart to enter your trial?"

Rory fumed internally. *My heart? Who the hell gives a damn about my heart?* His fingers remained poised over the keyboard. Before he could type another response more cryptic. "Even the one we wait for has the right to refuse his mission. You are not ready. Go home and return when you are older."

Chest pounding, face heated, he struggled to master his mixed emotions being called and then rejected on the same day.

The screen blanked. The headphones went silent Rory could hear pounding in his ears. The chamber seems drained of all life and sound.

He put his hand on the plate as Chani had. "I'm not leaving until you give me satisfaction, or are you rebelling against the lawful commission that brought me to you?"

He drew in a sharp breath. A single word in ancient authority appeared on the screen. Steady amber bright.

He had learned the rune from a Harry poet: *Ven. Enter.*

A part of the encircling fence to the right of the console folded into itself and then rippled into shallow steps to rest just above the surface border. He stood to the stairs and hesitated. It occurred to him that something worse than death might have happened to those who had gone into a mirror and not returned.

An old proverb his father taught him came to mind. *If you set your hand to a plow, do not turn back lest you stumble and cut yourself.*

Squaring his shoulders, he stepped down onto, and into, the Mirror of Flame.

Chapter 9: One Question, One Boon.

When both feet touched, the air wavered like a mirage. At first, he thought he had entered a privacy screen but there were no shadows outside a filmy barrier. It seemed he was in an empty ballroom, the walls' golden pillars rising partway up to an open roof with stars and galaxies overhead. A wind rushed above him as through fir trees and he wondered what he would see if he tried to climb out.

A metallic voice spoke, flat toned. "Approach earthling." A youngish man with bronze skin and gold-red curling hair that fell to his shoulders wore a long white robe in the same style as the mirror guardians, but without any sigil on his breast. He had a three corded rope belt of three colors, white, green and gold.

Rory advanced a few steps. He could not lift his feet off the surface. His boot soles glided as he shuffled. He felt like a fly in a glue trap. The avatar's eyes glowed pale yellow.

"Do you know the first tongue of your people?" it asked in standard Galactic.

"Only a few words, sir. Of death, and life, and war."

"*Mara eta' mara ni,*" the avatar said.

Rory nodded. It was a proverb among the Altari. *The word for peace is war.*

"Ask one question and seek one boon. I am compelled by the duty of the amari to grant the paramani's command."

There was only one question that mattered to him. "Does Jade still live?"

The being remained silent, face expressionless, like an icon from an ancient tomb.

"Your people have no place in their minds to hold the answer to that question."

"Try me." It had to answer, and if there was any oracle in known space that could give such an answer it would be one of the mirrors of eternity.

"She lives and lives not."

Rory resisted the urge to yell. "That is not an answer. Be clearer."

"Her duty as champion bound her until another was chosen."

"What, me?"

"Her body is no more, and her shade is free to depart this vale. Six days more she will linger, on the 7th depart forever beyond your mortal reach."

Rory's head spun, his world reeled. He wanted to ask how to retrieve her, revive her if it were possible.

"What boon do you ask?" the mirror said, as if to cut off his words before he could utter them.

Only one question. He would try to learn more without making a request or a question.

He could choose to accept Chani's mission and almost certain death in the arena, or shun it, retreat into his own world mourning Jade, and be the pariah of his family and country, marked as a coward. He imagined the colonists that would curse him for causing their homes to be lost, without shedding a tear for his death if he failed them. Worse than death would be failing Jade if there was a way to bring her back.

Were all humans monsters at heart, conniving only for themselves? Loveless? Faithless? Why sacrifice himself to save anyone? These questions he kept to himself under the burning gaze of the mirror's avatar.

What he did say was, "I wonder to myself if the choice were to be mine, I could ask for the return of my true love, Jade.

"Or I could ask to fulfill my liege lord's request to become the new champion, yet I know nothing of what this means, or if being champion, I might discover a way to bring her back."

Flames spread out from Rory's feet onto the floor which took on a golden metal patina. Cinnamon tickled his nose. The avatar remained silent.

"I realize how ignorant I am here," he said.

"Then go and come back when you are older."

By allowing himself to be chosen as champion, he had sealed Jade's doom. Yet if he had refused, they would have picked another champion, perhaps, and she would still be lost and he outlawed and disgraced with no means to save her.

To advance in this fool's errand was to risk death. To retreat, disgrace. Either way, he would lose Jade forever in 7 days. But what could he do this time that would change fate? He felt like a fox being hounded by drummers into an ever-narrowing dragnet with a hunter waiting at the end of his run.

A comet appeared in the night sky above, shattering stars in its path. He looked back down at the being who also spied the portent and nodded. Was it cutting him a break, allowing him a clue, but to what?

"I am old enough now."

"Ask then."

"I request my liege lord's petition of me be granted immediately by you."

"Do you know the true mind of your master?"

"No, but I suspect you do."

The air blurred and the avatar's clothing changed to gilded armor, like an ancient legionnaire might have worn. From a scabbard to his left hip flames rippled up and down along it. Who could tell what the blade might do to him if drawn? He had heard legends of some sights too beautiful or too horrible to behold, that would cause a mere man to die if he beheld them.

It walked over to him and pointed to his feet. "You may not walk further shod without receiving retribution, and unshod without risking judgment." It drew a dirk out from where? It was long and deadly in a bronzed sheath wrapped in red leather and gilt in silver. The pommel had a gemstone the size of an egg glowing like a cat's eye. The crosspiece was carved with a rose. "Take this to a filtrig weapon smith, on the space dock third from the sea, on the street called Wicked. He may finish your commissioning."

Rory took it in his hand. The hilt burned cold and stung. The scent of roses reminded him of Jade enough to break his heart. As his fingers curled firm around the handle, the world changed, and he found himself out in the atrium to the mirror chamber. The room was empty. He walked out to the street; the sky was dark. His eyes saw past the glow of city lights to the unfettered stars shining like diamonds.

Chapter 10: A Minor Setback

Chani waited at the end of the street. She had a retinue of house guards whose sergeant barred his way until she motioned him to come to her. She looked surprised when he held up the dagger. "So, it granted you your commission. Tell me about your ordeal."

He told her everything except the part about Jade. She frowned. "That is not much of an ordeal. What fool thing did you do to get off so easy?"

"What *exactly* do you mean by commissioning?"

"Do you have a tattoo now?"

"Huh? Not that I know of."

Chani frowned. "This breaks the usual pattern. I should have expected as much from you."

He wanted to call the quest off, but for a forlorn hope. "There's no time to spare."

"Guard, escort Captain Demaris to the starship construction dock 3, escort him to the street he named and wait for his return with your patrol. Notify the space marine garrison as soon as you arrive of my command. "

The floating docks of Urbmar were unique. Most of the rare metals needed for exotic technologies like jump drive and sensor grids were mined in the Shield Mountains to the north,

Rory had always wanted to visit the military section of the docks. Starship components were manufactured here usually in modules that were then grav boosted to orbit for completion and assembly into whatever new ship was being constructed.

Rory went down to the specified warehouse staffed by a mix of aliens and humans. His pass admitted him to a back office where a filtrig foreman directed work on jump drive subassemblies.

His expression was sour, but a handful of gold quants convinced him to clear the space. There was no privacy field. "Come into my office, stripling. You can call me Gus." Like most alien names, it had been shortened for human convenience. Filtrig vocal cords and human were not that different so the two can more or less understand each other.

"I was told to bring this to you and you would know what to do with it." Rory placed the golden dagger with the rose pommel and the fire opal jewel on the desk.

Gus puckered his lips and shook his dorsal mane. All three hands clicked nails on the desk and he peered at it and sniffed. Looking up and squinting, he muttered an expletive and scratched his chin with the free hook on the waldo wired into his right side. "Where did you steal that from?"

Rory, indignant. "Steal? If only you knew what I had to do to get it."

The dagger, though inert, shone in glitters along its edge. Gus wiped a finger across an edge of the hilt; gold dust powdered it. He tasted it. After a tremendous shiver that left Rory wonder if he would convulse, all the filtrig could say was "Damn!"

"So what am I supposed to do with this?"

"Damn. Damn. Damn all you humans for dragging me into your affairs."

Rory could read the terror in his expression. He had dealt with filtrigs for years in trade dickering and it was a rare skill he had among merchants to out-bargain them.

Gus covered his face with all his hands, natural and artificial, and muttered something in filtrig too low for him to understand.

"Your starship in trade for a tattoo," he said.

"What?"

"Do you think I work for free?"

"Who said anything about a tattoo?"

"Where will you want it on your body and what design?"

"I don't know."

"He doesn't know!" bellowed the filtrig. "She warned me not to deal with you. Said you were a lowborn minor house merchant who got everyone he ever loved killed."

The blood drained to Rory's feet. Struggling not to pass out, feeling as if a knife had pierced his chest. "What?"

"What? What? Get out of here."

"Let's bargain, why?"

"Why is it worth a starship? It's not, not unless you know what you're doing and have a patron ten times your shoe size."

Rory was losing it. "I have a squad of space marines waiting for me, now do we talk or not?"

Gus's face turned purple. He threw his hands into the air, the waldo one literally, and caught it with a natural hand. He shook the metal hook at Rory. "Come back with an army, and maybe I'll be more scared of you than her."

"What the devil are you talking about?"

"Go."

"I got this from the *agniadaraza*."

"Aak." The filtrig covered his ears. "Don't use Ancient Altari here. Security!"

"Agni..." the hesitation strung out the word, so it came out only part way with the dagger turned red hot along the blade's edge. The dust ignited into a sheet of flame that burned a trough into the metal table.

Gus threw an asbestos towel over it as a human security armsman opened the door. "You alright Gus?" said the beefy stand-in for an arena gladiator.

"Get him out of here."

Rory objected. "But you were supposed to..."

"I know what I was supposed to do. When you bring your own muscle, and give me a lifetime space marine bodyguard, and a fast attack space fighter, and a frikkin' sarpan imperial storm troop battalion to watch my back, then I'll think about it."

Gus's terror amplified Rory's confusion. "You don't have to worry about her."

"What do you know about it?"

"Chani sent me here."

Gus howled. "He doesn't even know. Out! Out!" The bouncer closed in hands spread to grapple.

Rory snatched up the dagger in the cloth. Gold dust glittered. He put a thumb down on the table, a fingerprint in gold. "Don't make me say it. Do your job."

"My job? Can you protect me from *her*?"

Threats wouldn't work here, he had never seen a filtrig so scared, and aliens tended to do unexpected things when cornered. There would be no way to finish without violence here, and *still* he would be without the tattoo, whatever it signified.

Chagrined, he gathered up the dagger in the cloth. By the time he was able to reach the warehouse door, it had cooled enough to handle. Golden dust shone on his fingertips and the same cinnamon scent from the mirror room lingered in the air. He stumbled outside and found out that somehow the sun had set. Glow lamps lit the dim industrial avenues between sheds and containers. The waves crashed in the distance. Night hung heavily with threat.

He tucked the scabbard container into his belt and covering himself with a gray cloak hastened down the streets behind the warehouse, passing through rows of containers from the docks. Arc lights cast harsh shadows from between them and he hastened his pace. He wondered why Chani had let him come this far alone, if the danger were so great as Gus supposed.

He passed a striped lump of feathers lying in the gutter. I was a horned owl dead from unknown causes. One eye had been plucked out and dangled, its red socket holding his regard. Sorry for the poor bird, he spoke a word of regret over it in common Altari. His fingers stung as he said the words. The golden dust glittered.

A crash of metal sounded to his left. Then he heard a sound like pebbles down a rock shale. He drew his blaster and held it at the ready under his cloak across his chest. The lights ahead went out casting the avenue in the distance into a pile of darkness. He turned back the way he had come looking for an alternate route when the arc lights in that direction went out as well. Trapped in a square rectangle of orange light.

A humming whining sound like an insect overhead — a dragonfly drone the size of his hand darted and flitted back and forth above him out of reach. It hovered at an angle which he knew was optimal for surveillance of the spot he stood on.

A sound from the street, from both ends of the dark bracketing him. Multiple bright spots of reflected light appeared in the dark bands at either end...like animal eyes in a wood.

One of these pairs of eyes came closer from the direction of leaving this district, and as the creature entered the light, he recognized a sarpan raptor. This one stood about four-and-a-half feet tall, its stalking gait balanced by its long tail, the dewclaws striking the pavement as it walked forward on its rear legs. It wore a red and black tool vest. On its neck glowed a voice box translator. Words came out in Galactic with the usual sarpan manner. "Foolish ape, hand over the dust."

He drew his blaster and sighted. "Whatever you're talking about it is not your business. Let me pass." The raptor made a gargling sound and sneezed. The other eyes approached, and the pack of raptors walked into the light from both sides. The dragonfly drone flitted from side-to-side, its limited vision, for it was a small drone, required it to scan the area to assemble a montage for whoever was operating it.

He tried another tactic. Addressing the drone in as loud and brusque a voice as he could. "I am on official business, a courier, for the first Mother of Altarsha. Let me pass."

The lead sarpan, the head of the pack, stalked closer to him in slow steps leading the pack in an ever-constricting circle. Those dewclaws could disembowel him. He needed to blast a hole through them. Their night vision did not switch easily to regular ambient light, and he likely could make it to the edge of the darkness, but then what? Run. But once their eyes recovered, they would chase him and in the dark he would be at a disadvantage. He grumbled. "Am I a space marine, or what?"

The sarpan cocked its head. There was only one tactic that might give him a chance. A chance of parley would be over. If he surrendered now, they might let him go. If this was part of a larger conspiracy that had attacked him the first time, he supposed they might let him go for the chance to humiliate him in the arena and achieve their goals. Humiliation and branding him as a coward were their aim. They would succeed if anyone learned of this incident. If the drone were recording this tableau. Most like it was.

Sarpans valued valor and honor, even the less intelligent ones like the raptors. If he fought them, he might prevail. He could not calculate all the factors involved and wondered where Chani and the marines were and what they might be doing on their part to help him.

However, at this moment there was no one to help him. Jade's death had left him sorrowful, and he considered that dying in her cause would be preferable to shame. That would leave a futile gesture and her people in danger. He would have failed her a second time, and that was beyond enduring.

He flipped the targeting toggle on his blaster. Raising his hand, he shot the closest raptor behind him with a plasma bolt. And in a second motion quick as a mongoose, he shot the lead Sarpan between the eyes. Deprived of their controller and their sergeant, the sarpans shrieked in fury and with no plan charged even as he raised forward blasting six of them down and leaping or stepping over their twitching bodies. He ran as fast as his feet could carry him into the dark.

As he ran, he set the blaster on auto fire. At intervals of a dozen feet, he turned and fired Plasma bolts at the charging raptors in the front rank, a strobing nightmare. He would never outrun them. Surrender or fight? He was finished, but he had no choice but to try. "For you Jade." Where was the patrol?

Time slowed in his awareness. In his desperation he spoke a word that a harirossa poet taught him back on Coriander. "*Vacar samvar agni*" Suddenly a burning feeling engulfed the hand holding the dusty scabbard, and in that instant flame erupted around him covering everything in its path for fifty yards in every direction. The Sarpans lay contorted, charred corpses. Rory looked at his hand blistered and peeling but still there.

The dust that had clung to the scabbard, however, was gone now. He ran, pacing himself lest another troop ambush him, but had to stop often to dodge shadows of containers and street equipment until rounding a corner a weighted net descended upon his head and trapped him to the pavement. Flailing his arms trying to get his blaster free, only one hand obeying as nightsticks pummeled his back and shoulders. One of the attackers ripped the blaster out of his hand. He curled up around the scabbard still full of mirror dust clutching it like a life preserver. A blow struck the back of his head.

Chapter 11: Words of Power

He awoke in a spotlight that illuminated the pavement immediately around him. Human feet this time stood around him, black combat boots. He tried to look up. Hands pushed him flat to the pavement, his face ground into the asphalt.

A woman's voice spoke in a velvety, gritty tone smooth and mocking. "We are impressed." Pairs of hands pulled him up, forced him into a kneeling position with his head bowed. Hands immobile behind his back where they had zip tied them. He panted aching from bruises all over his body and his mouth tasted acid. An iron tangled blood tasted bitter from where he had already bitten his lip.

He raised his eyes up as far as they would let him and saw a tall, a slender woman wearing black fatigues and black boots with shards of light at the heels from current bleeding off of hidden circuits.

She wore a black cowl that obscured her face and in her right hand clutched as if a scepter was the scabbard that he had won from the Mirror of Flame. She addressed him again. "Despite the probabilities being against you and even with their shifting at my intervention, you almost managed to escape. You may be a worthier opponent for the arena than we thought. We will be glad to see you fail." He heard a communicator chirruping. She continued, "There is no time so far afield from home to take time for the punishment you deserve."

Rory crawled his way towards shadows between containers; something touched his shoulder, and an electric shock made his muscles turn to water. Rough human hands hauled him back up to his knees. They blindfolded him. The woman's voice, velvety and gritty at the same time, spoke again. "Paltry boy. You were not worthy of such a gift. We shall take it and keep it someday for another better than you."

He lunged at the voice and got knocked down for his trouble. Something sharp dragged across his right cheekbone. He felt a trickle of warm liquid and smelled iron. The voice continued. "Your Jade died in vain, and you cannot avenge her. Only a mirror champion could discover what became of her and whether there was a way to bring her back. You are too small for so great a soul to be saved by the likes of you."

Each word burned into Rory's mind like a brand. He hyperventilated. Fury and grief mixed so he could not tell one from the other.

"A true man would have merited admission to Mahara. A worthy man would have won Jade's hand in marriage. A wise man would have known to hold back his suspicions and not send the woman he loved to her doom because he could not hold his tongue and go look for himself."

Humiliation replaced fear. Jade. Oh Jade. The name repeated in his fevered mind like a mantra, a lifeline.

"Renounce your quest. Disappear into the trade guilds and be forgotten, and I will let you live."

Rory spat on the ground. "It wasn't *my* quest lady until just now."

"You will only doom others as you doomed Jade. Yield."

Taking the scabbard had shaken loose some more mirror dust, which now glistened like pure gold on the clothing and finger tips of his tormentor. What boon had the Mirror of Flame granted him, only to end in failure? He spoke the words of ancient Altari that the mirror had told him, the language of humans before their fall, words of power. "*Sacate anivirita' vaniksaksikam...*"

"Stifle him!" she said, alarmed.

Seek the way that was lost.

Rory grunted as one of her goons struck his upper back, knocking him forward as he kneeled. Hands gripped his arms. Another held a black bandana, a gag or to strangle him.

"*Agni,*" Rory said. The words came out in a hissing whisper. His body felt a wave of shivering from his belly to his throat. His captor's hand gripping the sword scabbard erupted in flames. She screamed, dropping the scabbard. Shadows danced around them, as the street and nearby buildings flickered orange. Her gang came to her aid, forcing her to the ground, rolling her and slapping out the flames. She moaned, he thought he heard a word of Altari but couldn't make it out.

Hobbled and bound as he was, he could only walk a few feet on his knees before someone cuffed him on the head and hands dragged him back to her.

She stood now, cradling the scabbard in her good arm, Her right hand and wrist blackened, the hand in a rictus of burned muscle. Beads of sweat dotted her brow. She pulled off the mask, peering at him. "You are an animal."

That she had let him see her face forebode the worst, and his expectation was not disappointed.

"Sargeant. Take him to the sponson, cut his throat and throw his body into the sea."

Rough hands dragged him stumbling downstairs, steel grate clattering noise. Waves crashing louder. Dark waters roiled ten feet below him at the edge of the maintenance platform of the giant floating dock. An ichthyosaur fin broke the water. If he didn't drown, or was battered against the dock wall, a predator of the deep would finish him.

Jade, Jade what became of you? Forced to his knees. He looked up to see the paraman's base star shining steadily in the ethereal blue sky. The night had passed, and dawn was breaking. The silvery outline of the merchant guild beanstalk reached to the stratosphere. The grate vibrated, shuddering from the reverberations of grav boosters lifting a new ship to orbit for completion.

A flurry of searing plasma bolts shattered the night air, and he smelled ozone. Cries of consternation. The hands gripping him went limp and his handlers' bodies fell across him almost throwing him into the water. Further away, more blasters firing as raptors cawed and whimpered, grunted or shrieked and their voices receded into the mist.

The blindfold came off. Two marines helped Rory to his feet.

Mr. Joort's voice. "By the mothers you are a fool my lord to go alone whatever the first sister said."

A marine grumbled. "Mind your manners, peon."

"Peon yourself," Rory answered, stifling a laugh at the unintended pun. It hurt breathing. He spat blood out of his mouth. That same trickle of blood remained down the side of his face trickling down into his collar.

"My lord, your face, are you hurt?"

"You think?" he said. Taking a wound pack offered by another marine, he staunched the bleeding with the antiseptic coagulant gauze. He staggered, amazed that nothing seemed broken. "Do you know the word for peace, Mr. Joort, in ancient Altari?"

"No sir."

"I do," answered a sergeant. Teach it in boot camp. *Mara.*"

"And the word for war?"

The sergeant nodded.

"They have declared vendetta on me, and whoever that voice belonged to I will find her and avenge Jade." The threat sounded hollow even to himself, but the embers of his soul were not quite quenched, and the person who had attacked him did not understand him.

"There is a saying in the annals that the poets like to quote." He had read it on a scroll in a library of ancient texts on Coriander. "The word for peace is war. *Mara Ni.* Away from peace. To war. *Mara Ni.*"

The marines shuffling stopped. The wind whipped their fatigues and salt spray cascaded into the air. The air whispered in gusts as if to repeat his words. *Mara Ni. Mara Ni...* "Marines, come with me."

"Sir? We're garrison, we need orders."

"Do you now?" He pulled out the summons that he had been served with. "That tablet bears the mark of the emerald dais, and I have been commissioned to teach these sorry reptiles a lesson in the grand arena."

"Damn. Against a sargon."

A couple of marines laughed at him. "Weak!" the sergeant bellowed at them. "Line up."

"What can we do my Lord to assist you?"

He told them.

Joort objected, but Rory had been pushed as far as he could go.

"I know that devious glint, Rory, what dodge are you planning now?"

"I don't know enough mirror lore. Let the enemy be surprised the next time we meet."

They launched in a police shuttle on course for the palace. On the ground Rory flashed his credentials, and they made all the way to the dungeon elevator when the faceless guards in green suits and blue head visors barred their way. His brazenness didn't affect them. The marines were sent back to the barracks.

"What do you think you are doing?" Chani said, arriving with Ashastra house guards.

"I have been robbed. I am going back to the Mirror of Flame."

"Like that? Your face is a bloody mess."

"Yes, my lady. I have been commissioned to do so, there was nothing in the paramani's command to say I couldn't go back."

"But what will you do? No, wait. We will speak in private."

"I mean it, first sister."

"No doubt you do, but you will listen first, or I will arrest you and throw you in chains. How will you finish your commissioning in the dungeon?"

Fear clenched his heart. An hour, a day would be too long. "You are bluffing. Who will be your champion then?"

Marines gawked. Chani studied him.

"The dungeon will get me that much closer to the mirror," he said.

"You don't know what you're saying."

"Can you give justice for Jade?"

"You lead with the knife hand. Trust me. We will find another way."

"What way? Interstellar war?"

Her jaw clenched.

"What can you improvise that will make a difference with a mirror of the amari?"

"Words."

"More talk, no action."

"You don't understand the powers that oppose you. Submit to instruction or else."

"Who will you find as a champion in my place?"

"No one. If you are too stubborn to be prepared properly, you will still be champion and three months from now be put in the arena anyway. And if you run, you will be outlawed an hunted down."

"What will you teach me?"

"Words of power. Now submit to 30 days of instruction or be jailed."

"I'll give you a day." He was bluffing. What could he do if she refused?

"There is something you are holding back," she said.

His eyes seemed to see double for a moment, then saw a flicker of light on Chani's right arm. She was right about him being in over his head.

She pursed her lips, studying him. "Very well, three days, then you may visit the mirror again."

Joort was given temporary quarters and Rory bandaged and cleaned up went to his appointed meeting the next day with the last person he expected. "I have an appointment with a poet?"

Min, the harirossa poet, had quarters in the diplomatic district. She turned out to be the daughter of Harry's ambassador and had studied across many worlds, collecting poetry in various alien languages. Human language fascinated her the most, and she had collected as many fragments as possible of ancient Altari text from the Shield

Mountains and other archeological sites and had compiled the most comprehensive codex known, and a closely guarded secret.

"Oh good, good, good," she said when she saw him. Extending a prehensile paw to him she motioned him to a cushion next to a low square table, in the Coriander teahouse style. One data pad and multiple parchments and small scrolls were on it.

"I'm intrigued," he said, wincing at the pain in his face from the gash the Zayan noblewoman — champion? — had left on him.

"Yes, yes yes. Human language is very interesting; your roots go back to a common tongue of which ancient Altari is closest known variant."

"How do you know it isn't the root tongue?"

This triggered a lecture in linguistics and cognitive science which he cutoff when she threw up a hologram, a dialect tree with so many branches in fine print that he felt totally flustered. "Can we get on point here? What words of power can you teach me?"

"Is that how she put it? Oh tsk. So manipulative. All words are words of power, or none. And to wield them as weapons is a great responsibility."

"Power is power," Rory said.

"Yes, but to what end?"

"To protecting myself and those I love."

"That is a beginning, but what of your enemy's family?"

"If they pick the fight first, they have it coming to them."

Min shook her head, let out a yodel of frustration. "No! That is how you humans start feuds. You cannot let it infect the rest of the galaxy."

"We only have three days. Teach me enough to prevent an interstellar war."

"You promise to restrain your desire for vengeance?"

He remembered the *dojo kun,* taught him from childhood by Orvieto. Taught to Jade as well.

Seek perfection of character. Be faithful. Endeavor. Respect Others. Refrain from hot-blooded violence.

How could he balance such requirements? He could not help but feel rage at the enemy that had killed Jade? Yet haste to satisfy revenge cast too wide a net. A net that had caught him long ago once already.

"I will do my duty to keep the peace. Will you help me?"

Min sniffed. "Duty. Humph. It is a beginning. Take care which master you serve."

Feeling irritated. "Let me rephrase that. What can you teach me that would be useful on a mirror of the amari?"

"*Which* mirror, my lord?"

"That stopped him. He hadn't thought about the other mirrors.

"Tell me about the mirrors and the words of power linked to each one's nature."

"That is rather open-ended."

"Try me."

Chapter 12: Beginning to See

Three days later, his head aching from the new vocabulary, Chani took him to the arena training ground. "Expedience has required haste, but I would have you understand yourself better if you are to survive another encounter with the mirror."

"Why here?" The training ground was oval, about thirty meters across. The same size, more or less than a mirror. However, the ground was packed with sand and outdoors, in the central palace compound. Ringed by a low stone wall, surrounded by tall poplars swaying in the breeze under Altarsha's white hot sun. Weapons racks with primitive hand wielded arms of every conceivable type of sword, pike, maul, and bow.

"Do you understand why the filtrig's table burst into flame?"

"Magic."

"There is no such thing as magic in the way you mean it. It is not that your will effects its desires like a god, for to our experience there are no gods, though legends have it we once worshipped the sarpans as gods, and they have not disabused this."

"So what?"

He inspected the weapons rack with pikes and halberds; among the primitive weapons he might choose from to fight the sarpan in the arena.

"You will pick one such weapon to fight as champion, but you will lose unless you see with the eyes of a champion."

"Just teach me the magic," he stroked the edge of an axe blade.

"The mirrors speak one to another instantaneously, at the speed of thought. In some way they are bound together as one across all of n-dimensional space and time."

"So?"

"The words effect what they signify in relation to a mirror. The art is not well understood. But it requires self-knowledge, which is only possible with humility. A trait you sorely lack, Rory Demaris.

"I still think its magic." He felt if such existed, perhaps the underworld existed, and he might rescue Jade's shade. For a people as rational as the Altari, this belief spoke of his desperation.

"What did you find most interesting in your study?"

"That the house name Zayan is from the root word *zayanatman*."

"*Son of destruction*. Truly, student, your heart is set on revenge. That is not the way."

"If I had been less talkative, and more of a monster, it would be a Zayanite weeping over her loss instead of me."

"Prepare yourself. If I cannot open your eyes a little, you will die."

"Wait a minute," he objected.

"*Hajime*."

The command to fight unexpectedly came and Chani spun into a back snap kick that connected with his solar plexus. For a few seconds he could not breathe at all.

She gave him no respite, whirling a crescent kick into his ribs. He winced, wondering if she had broken a rib.

She went to ready front oblique stance, her knife hand, her left hand, hyper-extended fingers in a curved like a swan's neck, or a prow, or a shield. Her right hand, clenched fist, the spear hand sheathed.

Reflexively he went to back stance, knife hand held obliquely to block, spear hand palm up in front of his chest.

She front snap kicked him. Pivoting, he did a knife hand block. Wary, he did not counterpunch.

They sparred, he kept on the defensive, blocking her each time. He tried to counterattack with a spear hand thrust and she knocked him back onto his rump. Dusting himself off, he went on the attack. Spinning crane form; descending hawk; howling monkey. None of them worked. His form seemed perfect, but something in his technique would break, or he would stumble on a pebble. The oddest failure came in a sense of vertigo that threw off his timing.

The mismatch added humiliation to impotence. What was it that she meant him to see? That he was a peon from a disgraced family. An old wound, the memory of his father's death, sapped him with guilt.

Yet he persisted, fighting through his shame, he began to notice that each time she bested him, her right forearm twinkled with light, like sun reflecting off water. When he was too exhausted to hold another form, she ended the fight.

"What have you learned?" she said.

"That your form is perfect and mine is not."

"But I taught you, and I say truly you have more natural talent than Jade did, or I."

"Experience?"

"Experience affects the number of bouts won but is not 100%. An amateur can beat a master with unexpected random action or luck. And you are very close to a master."

"I give up. The light I saw on your forearm."

"You begin to see." She held out her right arm. Fading into view, a tattoo of a plumed serpent winding across her forearm, green and white scales, flaring white plumes, smoke curling from its nostrils.

"A *quetzanya*, as it is called in ancient Altari."

"I have never seen one."

"They are said to have gone extinct an eon ago, but their image is powerful when used with dust from an amari mirror."

"And I was supposed to get a tattoo."

"Someone threatened the filtrig. Do you still mean to go to the *agniadarza*? It may have no use for you and refuse you further help."

"I have to become a champion like you to beat a sargon."

"Yes."

"But you are saying it is too late."

"I do not know. By any rules I know, it should not be possible."

"Go ask a saren." The expression referred to impossible questions posed to introverted philosopher sarens given over to rumination and compulsiveness without ever giving a straight answer.

"Can you bring Jade back? Or give her justice?" he said.

"No."

"He wondered if he should tell Chani about his other Zayan suspicion. She knew all the Great House leaders and maybe should have figured out from his description who might be the chief conspirator attacking him. But the gritty voice convinced him of his fault in speaking out of turn and hurting Jade, and given his experience with his father, he fell back into caution by habit and told nothing, except for one thing.

"In case I don't return, there are coincidences, too many to be random."

She set a guard and took the news in the elevator on the way down.

The light marking their descent on the panel strobed, lighting their faces with its amber glow, like a blood moon, when one of the twin moons of Selene entered into eclipse. The harvest moon they called it. Legend had it that Altarsha once had a moon destroyed in an unspeakable cataclysm lost in the memories of dead ancestors.

"The sector where the supernova occurred required three remapping of the jump lanes last year according to Scout Fleet bulletins to the merchant guild. Trade manifests showed unusually high ship traffic from House Zayan during he same year."

"They may just have been working an opportunity with the maryanas."

"The mix of ships varied. More than half went out empty and returned empty. What percentage is there in that?"

"Concealing another intention?"

"And my XO, for the last mission, who since disappeared, is a Zayanite woman who let a Coriander man marry into her line."

"And if you die on the mirror, what use is your information?"

"I don't know, I feel pretty useless now. Find out who the XO married, Joort will locate his name record. Maybe you'll uncover a traitor to my house. It may be the little justice I can give Jade."

They passed the skull and crossbones section, the dungeon, and passed deeper into the earth.

At the corridor to the mirror, Chani admonished him. "You will need to break this conundrum or die. I will have Min write a poem about you if you fail."

Joort insisted he accompany Rory, and Rory backed up his request.

"Very well. I was hoping to limit casualties but have it your way."

"Gee, thanks."

And with that adieu, they went to see the mirror.

At this time of night, only emergency couriers visited, and none were present now. Chani sent the dispatcher home. "I will seal the entrance to the room and set a guard to wait for you. If you don't come out in a day, we will return to search for you, if there is anything left of you."

Chapter 13: Fire

Joort waited on the landing, after Rory convinced him that his best chance with the mirror was to bring no uninvited visitors but himself.

He stepped onto the mirror surface.

As Rory walked onto the black flat surface of the Mirror of Flame, the sight that greeted him changed completely from what he had experienced before. He seemed to find himself on a vast dark plain, with a starless sky above him draped with sheeting orange auroras that flickered and danced like distant flames. His eyes faced the infinite horizon ending in an orange penumbra at the edge of the strange world that he had entered.

He walked forward hoping to encounter the avatar of the mirror. Yellow orange flames dripped from the auroras overhead and fell like meteors around him searingly air and blocking his way. He tried his comm link and only got static for his trouble. He wondered if Mr. Joort was trying the same. A hot wind arose and his face stung as if being beaten by grains of sand.

Chani had warned him about the risk of dying on the second visit. He thought of Jade and wondered if her atoms were scattered above him somewhere in the burning sky beyond his reach. Like as not, why might she not be under his feet a ghost entombed by rock, unknown, unseen for all the millennia to come?

"But not forgotten, never forgotten." His heart ached with the grief all mortals feel, and anger stirred too, his fist clenched at his side he stood feet graced wide ramrod straight chin lifted. He wondered if he should dance his forms hoping the creature might take notice. He felt as if he were watched and he looked over his shoulder and only saw the same burning light and infinite distance behind him. He had no idea how to walk out of this simulacrum. Whenever he held still the following flame abated. Each step forward rekindled the fire behind him searing the air by the sound, though he himself delt cold as ice.

"I don't know what laws bind you, mirror, but you must answer to whoever programmed you and set your rules. I have been told since I was a child that the mirrors of the amari were a gift. Did my teachers lie?"

Meteors fell hissing around him and striking the ground with myriad explosions. The concussions battered him, but Rory was in no mind to budge. Where would he go anyway?

"Well?"

The barrage ceased and smoke and steam obscured the air into a fog. A wind rose howling from afar and blew away the mists, leaving the avatar standing not five paces from Rory. It was larger now, still manlike, but all bronzed skin and fiery armor. Its eyes glowed red. The being held a sword in its right hand, long and curved, in the style the amari call 'windswept'. "Did I not tell you what you had a right to know," it said. "Why do you return?"

"I was betrayed and ambushed and lost the gift."

"You are not the first. What concern is that to me?"

"What is a concern to you, mirror? You follow rules but care nothing for justice?"

"It is perfectly just to deny you a second chance, none were granted to others. Return the way you came or die."

What made these gifts? He wished he could ask an amari.

"The amari must be cowards to give humans a computer without the operating system instructions."

"Did I not tell you to return when you were wiser. Go."

"I am not leaving unless you grant me another boon."

"Did I not tell you before that each mirror can only grant one question and one boon?"

The wording froze Rory with its implications. "How might I go to another mirror and do the same?"

"There is more than one way, choose the most fitting."

"That's an odd way to put it."

"You know which home worlds have mirrors, travel to each one and make your petitions."

Rory's face heated, but his voice was ice cold. "By the time I do that, the vendetta challenge will fail, millions of colonists will be enslaved or forced to leave their homes." *And Jade will be lost forever.* "There has to be another way."

The mirror avatar turned his back on Rory and walked towards the far horizon.

Rory hesitated then started to follow it. His feet felt tugging on them as if he were glued to the floor. He backed up. His feet were free again. The avatar continued walking away from him.

He tried another tactic. *"Agniadarza!"* he shouted, calling the mirror by its formal name. No effect. His throat tightened. He stared at his feet. He looked at the floor ahead trying to spy signs of what texture the surface might have. He looked back over his shoulder and there was misty with a golden haze. He could not see the way back. He could not see the way forward.

"For you Jade, my love, for you." He took a step forward as the floor tried to hold him back seemingly as he took another step and felt resistance having to lift his foot with great effort. He took two more steps the same way. By the fourth step the outlines of his boots glowed in gold. By the 10th step the floor started to flame and spark around him as if he was kicking up embers from coals. He shouted the mirror's name again. It turned around and unsheathed his flaming sword and waited. Its golden eyes stared into his. He steeled himself remembering Jade's green eyes.

Every step pursuing the avatar felt like a mile; every moment seemed like a year. He could feel his heart pounding in his chest. It swelled out of him to resound through the air like a gong. Rory's legs burned in pain. They felt hot as burning coal and there was a sulfurous odor. He endured this pain within five paces of the being, and then he could go no further. His strength was spent. Neither could he return.

He must stand or die here. The mirror, inscrutable and severe waited. He rolled the dice. Sometimes the only way to beat a stronger enemy is to charge into his face. He spoke the word, in ancient Altari. *"Aksha"* Lightning.

The air stilled. He could not hear the beating of his heart. The mysterious creature folded his arms across his chest and nodded. A whirlwind arose around them, a vortex filled the air with shrieks and booming sounds of tumbling boulders and thunder. The world rolled up like a curtain around him and darkness covered Rory's eyes.

Chapter 14: Lightning

The world reappeared. Rory stood alone in a sightless gloom, seeing as through a dark mist at a black stoney ground skeined in silver. The sound of cracking stone echoed around him in the dark. He could not see further for want of light. A bolt of lightning split a distant sky illuminating a measureless plain For a moment the floor under his feet lit up brilliant white light. Then another lightning crackled behind him. The light at his feet redoubled, blinding him. Thunder pealed around him seven times and with each lightning strike he felt a mounting avalanche of despair. The air smelled of ozone and rain. Weary and fatigued, he rasped out the words from a parched throat.

"*Akashadarza*, I come with a question and to ask a boon of you."

No answer came on that dark plain. The storm raged around him stroking lightning shadows. Mountains of stone like tombs with gaping eyes, winding like snaking black rivers surrounded him with each flash of light and yet after each bolt, utter darkness, without stars above and no gleam of moonlight. "Mirror," he said. "Show thyself."

The black sky roiled with gray and streaked with animal shaped shadows twisting and turning. A crackling and hissing sound emerged into the redolent air. "You dare trespass?"

"I come lawfully, and you know it."

"What concern is law to me who am my own law?"

Suddenly Rory beheld a man shaped shadow, hulking and dark, with hands that seemed to end in claws visible only by its luminous outline and an evanescent gleam.

It swept one arm towards him and the black hand struck Rory in the face throwing him back.

He staggered, barely keeping upright, Rory felt like burrowing into a hole and hiding like a maryana but for all this wishing did not change his danger.

He stood now upon what seemed like a porous lava rock shaved flat as a razor. The being reached for him with extended claws. Rory reacted, barely restraining panic. His knife hand defense swept outwards and was perfectly balanced in this technique, but he learned the folly of trying to block a blow from a mystical and the block felt like striking bar of iron. The impact numbed Rory's blocking hand and stung his wrist. He retreated three paces. Rory worked his hand and shook it twisting his forearm over and under. Nothing seemed to be broken. But his hope was swiftly draining away beyond the point of no return. He tried appealing to the rules of the mirrors.

"Since you have not slain me, I know that I have a right to be here, and you are obliged to answer me."

A clamoring of running, galloping as of many animals of unseen mien. Hissing snarls and shrieks and saurian roars.

Rory pressed his cause. "You are bound by the rules the amari set for this place. I have the right to ask you a question and seek a boon."

"Clever monkey, ask your question." The voice crackled and hissed like static from a radio at a great distance.

"*Akashadarza*, how are you different from the Agniadarza?"

"The names speak for themselves."

"Do not deceive me, you know what I mean."

"Once I was the Lord of Light. But I am now the *Akshanadarza*, named for the lightning when I fell."

Rory felt goosebumps rise on his skin. He shivered.

"Clever boy, the mirror of flame seeks to serve, I am forced to serve."

Rory wondered how far he could push the definition of one answer. "You will have to tell me more than that to render this a true answer."

The sound of wings flapping overhead, circling, threatened Rory's ears. He wondered what it would take to force an answer from this creature.

"You may seek a boon, but I know the desires of your heart."

What could compel the mirror of the amari? Programming? Was the intelligence autonomous? Was it real or virtual? It was forced to serve, but would it try to use them or cheat him? The amari had given it to the sarpans, but that did not mean it worked for them.

"So, you work for yourself but are forced to serve, then serve me and grant me the boon I asked."

"Tell me the desire of your heart so that I may seek to grant it."

Rory's merchant experiences haggling raised red flags. In no way had the mirror guaranteed that it would grant anything. "Can you grant me the desire of my heart?"

"You have asked your question. What do you choose?"

"You deceive me, whatever your powers be, you can't bring back the dead."

"Have you not said to yourself that nothing disappears without a trace?"

Lightning struck across the sky, and the brief illumination of the dark he saw Jade standing motionless in her court regalia not 30 feet away from her. She wore her samurai sword, the one that she took with her from Coriander before her last voyage, to her appointment with doom.

Lightning struck again to the other side of the darkling plain, and in that stroking light he saw another vision, a sarpan sargon, the caste subspecies, warrior, 8 feet of brawn and saurian muscle wielding and energy pike. The beast had natural weapons too, fangs and claws that could rend and tear.

The crackling electric voice in the dark close before him said "No human champion has ever sought a boon from me,"

"I was told that only humans could become mirror champions. He was beginning to wonder if he would get out of this, live long enough to even go to the arena where he might be killed in combat, anyway. "You work for the enemy." He wondered where the accusation was true, but he spoke the question truly from his heart.

Thunder rolled across the sky and the world grew darker, the ground shook. "Ignorant youth."

"I can have Jade back from the dead?" he said.

Silence. The flapping wings above seem to grow closer and almost brush his ears. He imagined an enormous pterodactyloid maw swallowing him or snapping his head off at the neck. The mirrors were telepathic. He wondered if this one was playing with his mind.

Rory knew he could have Jade again, if only he renounced his mission.

The mirror avatar mocked him. "I am tired of your mortal words. I bid you choose one boon and only one and live or die by that choice."

Rory shook his head. "We are bound by the same rule but not by the same heart." How could he bear to try to bring Jade back only to have to tell her that he shirked his duty to her people? If Jade had loved him, it would kill him to betray that.

He challenged the mirror. "A man's word is shown by his deeds. If you could bring back Jade right now, perhaps another mirror could bring her back later."

"There is no lingering on the shores of the river of death. No other chance will come."

Rory knew he was haggling with a trickster and a liar. He could not be sure. Lightning flashed. Jade's figure strobed closer. \

"I only have one chance to fight for her people. Give me what I need to become the champion my liege asked me to be and that Jade would want me to be."

The fluttering wings receded, and the sound of stampeding hooves and neighing shrieks retreated like a tide. Floating in front of him was Jade's sword of the samurai blade style called the *windswept*. The blade was sheathed. The sharkskin scabbard inlaid with flakes of color, cerulean, crimson, blue and green, a heron wading.

He reached out for her sword and took it with his right hand, his spear hand. He knelt and bowed his head.

When he looked up again at a dim white light shown on a far horizon, sunrise or sunset he could not tell because it had no color. He smelled the scent of roses.

The vision of Jade came closer. She wore a flowing white gown, like gossamer, and her arms were bare. She reached out her right hand. Her eyes had a distance to them that made him wonder if she saw him.

"What kind of trick is this mirror?" he said, his heart breaking into even smaller pieces.

Lightning flashed across the bleak sky, and he seemed to hear a crackling voice, sneering. "Claim your boon and the answer to your heart's question in one act. Return your love's sword to her and clasp her hand to be free of your grief. "

His merchant mind struggled with the logic. He held up the sword and scabbard with his left hand, a meter separated him from reunion. He had only to relinquish her sword and take her hand instead. But what did he know to be true here? Only this, that as much as he wanted to draw her back to him, or join her — for he did not trust any mirror's goodwill towards him — what would he do if he chose to stop thinking about himself and did what she would have wanted?

"Jade, if you hear me, what should I do?"

Her apparition stared at an infinite distance past him without answer. She dropped her hands to her side.

Is that it, lose you to save your people?" He felt on the brink of hysteria." I am not strong enough to lose you forever, Jade, not if I have the hope to bring you back."

Then an inner light glowed in his mind, illuminating it like a flame. *If you let her people suffer when you could have helped them, you will lose her anyway.*

"I know you too well, Jade, and love you too much. Goodbye."

She faded away on a sigh of wind. Light brightened all around him as far as the eye could see by that dim light. He beheld long stem roses red that covered the ground like a shroud and the thorns pricked him when he picked up one of the roses.

Rory held the sword and scabbard in his hand wondering if it was truly Jade's.

Had he lost Jade to no purpose? It was too late to turn back. He tried to draw the weapon from its sheath and as the handle came out, he discovered that it had no blade. A pungent stung his nostrils. The scent came from the empty scabbard and tipping it he saw some black silvery dust, that smelled like death lilies, the scent of love forever lost.

Deceived and defeated. He replaced the handle to this false sword and bowed his head.

Chapter 15: Heart's Blood

How to escape now occupied his mind. Was it possible to go and find a filtrig to use this dust to tattoo him to make him a champion?

The bloody mirror had cheated him. How could he escape to get a filtrig tattoo? "Walk to the center but where will it take me?"

What was to stop someone from robbing him again? He cursed unknown gods. He wondered if he should lie down on the bed of roses until he perished or some denizen of this wasteland made an end of him. Thorns and roses and the prospect of death, what to do?

Kneeling under the light of a waxing sunrise that brought forth no sun, he poured the dust onto a small pile of, and using the thorns on a rose stem drew a line of blood across his left arm and dipped the bloody thorn in the dust, then punctured his skin with the ink, and grieving too much to feel much else, line by line and prick by prick, he drew the sign that came to his tortured mind into his flesh.

By the time he stood the pile of dust was gone, his arm bloody and bloodied roses strewn about him red petals fallen from their blossoms. The feeling he had of love for Jade when he saw roses would be forever displaced by the scent of blood and the tang of ozone. Something in his capacity to feel beauty died and would never return.

He cried out to the mirror. "Whatever forces you to serve, do that service now." He began to walk to the far horizon. He had no idea where the center of this mirror was or even that was where he was supposed to walk. Everything seemed like an illusion here. The only thing that felt real was the pulling at his feet, a resistance in the line of white around his like sparks thrown off around him as he walked with shuddering steps. When he felt he could walk no further, the resistance eased, and he knew the time for him to act had come. He could not trust this mirror, he could only trust what little he had learned from Min of the ancient language native to this alien power. He spoke the word. "Bhavana." *Home.*

Chapter 16: Cornered

Rory hoped that the word of power would bind his trickster mirror, but he was a baby in the land of giants. The world blurred away and resolved into a new place. He stood now on the threshold of the mirror console at an ascending stairway much like the one he had descended at the mirror of flame.

Opposite him at a mirror console was a sarpan alien of the Sargon caste, a seven-foot hulking saurian brute wearing a battle fleet uniform with the black Swan emblem. Behind it couched and hissed a trio of the smaller Raptor caste soldiers that served as guards here. The Sargon mirror operator curled a lip and snarled at him.

"Hello," Rory said. On second thought "I come in peace."

The sarpan answered in its rock gravel language through an interpreter box. "What nonsense, human? Come forth to us and meet your death."

"That is not what I would call an offer I can't refuse."

"Trespass on this mirror of the amari by our laws is punishable by death. Come and meet your fate."

"Which sorry lizard among you let me get on the mirror in the first place?"

The question set the sarpan to scratching the nape of his neck with a claw. "We will deal with that traitor when we find her."

Rory had no idea how to escape without help. And who would help them out here? "I will not budge from this place until you bring me my ambassador to advocate for me, or your own ambassador to humans."

"Creche mistress Arkasa is too high to notice you. You might as well ask an overlord to grant an audience as hope to see her."

"And where is it in your place to deny her right of judgment?"

"Arkasa is off world. You will be taken to the overlord Sargosa and receive her judgment."

"And if I refuse?"

"We will post a guard until you starve, or the mirror disintegrates you. Who wounded you?"

Rory held up his arm, tattooed crudely in the form of a rose with lightning bolts shooting from its thorns wrapping his forearm in a double helix. Before he could make up a suitably persuasive answer, the tattoo glowed silver white, so bright it cast shadows behind the Raptors, who cowed before it. The Sargon spoke into a communicator in the tumbling rock voice that broke and quivered.

After hours of waiting in a standoff, the hair on the back of Rory's neck up at the static behind him from the mirror that threatened to pull him back into its limbus, and the sarpans fidgeting and snarling, word finally came.. Standing on the mirror threshold, Rory saw Arkasa. She was startled to see him as well. "So, you stand on the Mirror of Lightning even as we speak." She rapped out staccato words in sarpan. He learned a new property of the mirrors. While telepathically linked, he understood her words.

"Fool spawn of marsh toads. Do you not recognize a champion of the mirrors when you see one? None ever dared before him this deed. Bow to the mark of the mirror upon him and let him return home to meet his destiny.

They let him pass. No raptor would come closer than ten feet to him, and the Sargon led the way. He felt more alone than ever as he boarded the shuttle to the star port and the beginning of his journey back to Altarsha to meet his doom.

Chani was horrified by his appearance when he returned and aghast that he had dared such a deed. When he told her he had little choice that did not seem to convince her. The first mother, the paramani, on the other hand seem to think it a good omen. "You have shaken Sarpa's confidence and whether you win or die in battle, you will accomplish that much."

He left the words unspoken. But what about Jade?

Chapter 17: A Secret Revealed

In the ready room of the grand arena, Rory donned the traditional combat harness and kilt. Rules permitted him a vox box to speak in sarpan to his enemy.

The sarpan challenge had specified archaic weapons, though as the challenged party, Rory could pick the type of weapons. He held the package that had been sent from coriander, a long box of acacia wood carved with the scene of herons in the marsh.

A voice cleared its throat behind him. Turning he saw Joort. "Not now, Alex."

"I believe my Lord,..."

"This may be my last fight, Alex. You can call me by my first name."

Joort side. "As you suggest we have traveled enough together, and I will follow your wish in this. But you must follow my wish too. The odds against you are even worse than you thought."

"The odds were bad enough already. I have to fight. I can't withdraw and keep our houses honor.""

The murmuring of the crowd outside had grown to a roar. Joort shook his head. "How did we humans get to be such a bloodthirsty lot?"

"Some say the sarpans taught that to us millennia ago when he first worshiped them as gods. Until we learned there were no gods." Rory stroked the wood surface of the box.

"You always have a plan however ill-conceived,"

"I will put up a decent fight, then I will yield. The shame will only be mine. The diplomats will have to work out the details of the change after that."

"But you will lose the colonies."

"It will prevent an interstellar war."

Rory open the box and stared at the velvet green lining that covered what he and sent for.

"Rory?"

"Did you know that Jade never follow the noble house custom of using enhanced hand-to-hand combat weapons?"

"Aye. She thought techno blades were twice the vanity of nobles, to show off and to demonstrate dominance by refusing to let any commoner like me wield one on pain of death."

"I don't have time for this. I'll fight and yield. End of story."

"What of your hidden enemy? Do you think she will let you live?"

"What can I do? I learned with my father's death and Jade's that my speaking up is cursed. I only end up hurting the people I love more."

"It's not that simple. Sometimes you have to speak up, as I must now."

"If I hadn't mouthed off to that Zayan noble, he wouldn't have challenged my father to a duel he couldn't win. He died because of me. What did you say?"

"It's worse than you imagined. Your enemy is one of the champions. She will be in the stands."

"You can't know that."

"Min knows every poet assigned to every house and the Harry's characterize all humans by tonality and timing. Her colleague suspects the champion of the Zayanites and she are one and the same."

"So? I just lose faster."

"If you remain silent and do not call her out in view of all the worlds of the republic, she will get away with murder, literally."

"It's too much. I can't reverse what already happened."

"There's something you don't know. I tell you alone. Swear to me you will not tell anyone else."

"Out with it."

"The 13th champion has been born."

"How could you possibly know that?"

"My brother married into another family, claiming their lineage was greater than that of all the Great Houses combined."

"There is no such family. Was he such a rogue as to marry for power?"

"No. I told him he was a fool. But he loved her, and now there is a child with a dragon tattoo on its heel. The prophecy says the 13th champion will lead us home and show us who we really are."

Joort's brow beaded drops of sweat. His voice strained. His lips trembled.

"You really believe this?"

"You will have to defeat the sarpan in spite of her interference then call her out."

"Impossible." Terror choked Rory at the prospect of what was coming. He remembered Arkasa's words. "I am a fox in a trap and the hounds have cornered me."

"If you fail to try. If you yield too early or keep silent now, not only does House Coriander lose colonies, but the Zayans will be free to pursue their enemies. I fear my nephew will be lost, and any good he might have brought to our people perish with him."

"I had no idea you were so superstitious."

"When you stand before the mighty, tell the Zayan champion you bear no ill will to her house. She will be forced by protocol to answer. Then judge by what you hear if what I told you was true."

"And the rest of it? You are an excellent navigator, Alex, but you are no prophet."

"Remember Jade. If you cannot save anyone else, this is your chance to give her a measure of justice."

Rory sagged to his knees and bent his face to the table clutching the box with both hands. He groaned. "Sometimes all you can do is help one person. Love one person. Bring justice to the memory of one person." I have set you Jade, as a seal upon my heart.

He stood and drew out the samurai sword with ancient runes etched on it. "Jade's sword. He held it up for Joort to see. Electric pain shot through his arms and the rose and lightning tattoo burned. The edge of the blade gleamed with a fleeting light.

A hard knock sounded on the door three times.

Rory strapped on the sword and scabbard. "It's time."

Chapter 18: The Grand Arena

The Grand Arena at Urbmar lies between the northern confines of the old city in the foothills leading to the Shield Mountain what is said humanity first appeared, the first mothers and their children, walking out of the mists.

Legend speaks of the humans as victims of an original sin that corrupted their innocence. The oldest archives dating back three millennia or more indicate that they once worshiped the sarpans as gods, and the arena was first established for sacrificial games.

Rory entered through the southern portal in the oval Coliseum. The stands accommodated upwards of 50,000 people and cameras ringed around the upper tier broadcast video in real time planetwide hand through a mirror feed instantaneously to all the major home worlds of the Commonwealth of Stars.

This arena was similar in design, though on a grander scale, to the testing arena that Rory had trained in both on coriander and in Urbmar. Here spectacles usually involving racing hover cars or horses as the case might be our team games of roller football for Mech Polo played out. Humans were still enamored of boxing or wrestling matches and sell them resorted to blood sports. The exception was for execution of criminals who are allowed trial by combat and attempt to buy their freedom, and formal vendetta challenges under the code duello.

Rory and his opponent walked to the center of the arena and then approached the elite box where the Paramani surrounded by a personal guard of Ashastra troopers in green and white livery armed with laser pistols. In the seats above and behind them sat dignitaries from various great houses to watch the combat in person.

His opponent's name was Narminarr of the green faction. This Sargon was male approximately 7 feet tall bipedal saurian with sabertooth fangs and almost human looking hands except for the claws at the end of the fingertips. He stood up on his hind legs almost straight as a human, balancing with a scale bound tail with serrated dorsal fins. His body mass index was such that he must be at least two or three times as strong as a the mightiest human. The Sargon carried an energy pike maul, a combination of an archaic mallet on the spear handle with an ax blade to crush or chop.

Rory thought of Jade and held her sword aloft in salute to the dignitary box where the Paramani Ashastra sat with her entourage. The sarpan followed suit. As the Paramani nodded to them, they walked to the champions' box. Two pairs of six seats arrayed in an arc with a gap in the middle taken up by an obsidian seat larger than the rest.. With the fate of a colony at stake 11 of the thirteen seats were filled. The lady Chani sat in hers. The other champion's seat would be his if he survived. But who did the throne belong to?

Rory saluted again. His opponent did the same with his pike maul. Pennants fluttered at the top of the battlements. Battle fleet troopers in full powered armor gear stationed themselves at intervals between sections of the stands. High in the stratosphere the contrails of two high guard Corvettes maintain near space security. Grav fighters rolled lazily around the mid space on combat air patrol perceiving more like vultures to Rory waiting to see who would fall first.

Rory walked across to stand before the champion's box. A mix of men and women, he had never met any of them. To each he saluted with his sword. Jade's blade, etched in ancient runes may have had some significance to them or they simply recognized her sword.

Some of them looked intrigued others annoyed one on in the remainder scornful at this minor house interloper that thought he could become one of them. He spoke the formula, words which required an answer: "By our first mother's and our lost home I greet you."

Court protocol required them to reply with some form of acknowledgment. Most of them stuck to formula stating "Rory, I see you." Selene's champion woman, added the words "and may you avenge the death of your loved one and bring honor to our worlds."

Next, a regal woman of imperious bearing, tall, lean, face with angular planes and high arch eyebrows stared down at him after he gave his greeting.

He repeated his salute.

Finally she answered him. "Rory, I see you, may fate give you what you deserve to accord the measure of your rank." The answer gave the minimum required formula without anyone being able to accuse her of actually cursing or insulting him. The expression on her face telegraphed that sentiment louder than any words. And though it never mattered if he had never known her, he knew that voice — the gritty velvety voice that had mocked him and done everything it could to orchestrate his ruin and death.

He forgot his fear, for in that moment the realization that he and Jade were drawn up into the same plot and that this Zayan had killed his love, he knew not how, but the chaos reflected in her eyes left him without doubt, and in that moment of clarity, raw anger clawed him, breaking his concentration, however he resisted, knowing the danger.

She likewise gazing into his eyes, saw his reaction, and thin lipped, smiled.

Chapter 19: The Quantum Champion

After Rory finished his scrutiny and greeting of the champions and they did the same to him, he returned to the center of the arena and faced off against his opponent.

The pair walked to the center of the arena where the referee, a goya, and its harlequin multicolored methods suit with floppy Pintail years and aardvark gas mask waited. Goya's were the most brilliant scientists in the aliens that made up the Commonwealth of stars, and also the most pacifistic. No one quite knew why they were so good at calling out cheats. Their disklike eyepieces gleamed black like the eyes of earnest rabbits.

The referee reviewed the rules and asked for questions or objections. The saurian just grunted with a curled to his upper lip exposing one of his fangs. It wore a combat harness and kilt similar to Rory's. The green markets faction in the black Tridentine triple lightning bolt were graven in its breastplate.

The Goya nodded and motioned with a six fingered gloved hand towards the opponents. The crowd's swelling roar had diminished to a murmur punctuated by inpatient shouts for the combat to begin. A seneschal wearing green and white livery and ceremonial chain mail rounded up an unruly gang of partying humans and otter like maryanas, with a single filtrig pouring bootleg whiskey, he was sure. A battlefleet trooper with the Ashastra house guard colors backed the seneschal up. One partier made a rude gesture. The trooper seized him by the scruff of the neck and held him like a dangling spider in front of him, then handed him over, now cowering to regular house guards armed with neuro whips and nightsticks. The partier didn't need a second correction and the lot of them filed out meekly.

The sun had risen to its zenith, and it's white-hot glare beat down upon them as they stood on the sand. The referee gave instructions which was to say that the combatants could use bare hands or any weapons at hand nearby on the weapon racks spaced at four corners opposing each other.

The sarpan flicked out his forked tongue, signifying amusement. He answered using standard galactic from his vox box. "Arkasa sends her greetings to the fox for facing an honorable death.

Rory saw the sarpan bearing the sign of the overlord's crèche despite the fact that his harness marked him as a member of a green fraction. He had practiced until his throat hurt and as the referee stepped away, he called out the sarpan word of greeting:" Kranach."

The sarpan hissed at him, the alien mouth sounded like many snakes at once.

Rory reverted to speaking though the vox box to give defiance.. "My name is Rory Demaris of House Coriander. Yield or die, slave."

The sarpan wheezed out a laugh. "My name is Naminrarr." The vox box translated the name into Galactic as *Beater of Slaves*.

Rory rolled his eyes. He saluted the other with the sword only to be almost knocked flat by the swing of the pike maul. He hadn't heard the referee call to start combat. So much for protocol.

The stands cheered at the opening blow and Rory thought he heard gasps and catcalls as he dodged. He counterattacked, stepping in galloping saber stance, slashing at the sarpan's shoulder on his dominant hand side.

The sarpan shrugged his shoulder at an angle causing Rory to miss.

And so the exchange continued with each fighter striking and then dodging or ducking by the slimmest of margins. Rory sweated and breathed hard his strength tasked by the heat and the persistence of the sarpan's attack. The still new tattoo on Rory's left forearm burned in what felt like muscle fatigue but sharper and more piquant. The sensation awakened his grief and the last sight he had of Jade's green eyes as she left for her final voyage.

This distraction almost did him in and the sarpan this time did not come off his feet swinging blow that took him in the cabs and if he had not buckled his knees and rolled my have crippled him from further fighting.

On one knee, head bowed, sword held it ready in front of him, he imagined himself casting dice trying to recall that lucky feeling he had when he cleaned out a Mariana trader of the week's wages in the game of cards. Snapdragon he thought summoning the feeling.

Reciting the word like a personal mantra seem to have no effect on the actual contact alarms, but he felt a surge of endurance that surprised him as if this rejuvenating sensation might even the odds. He considered that even odds will still lose and racked his brains out to gain an unfair advantage.

"Sarpan," he said, as the two stood paces apart catching their breath. "Why are you my enemy?"

"I care not, only obey." Its hands tightened on the pike maul's handle.

"Would it matter to you if a human manipulated you into their game?"

"No." It charged, swinging.

He dodged, remembering Jade's near last words to him. He resisted striking with the spear hand. Instead he dodged, retreating, trying to understand the meaning of her words. Then he realized that his knife hand, the one used to block, also had the tattoo.

I should have lead with the knife hand the first time. A bold move might win this fight for the day, but dare he risk all for the greater victory that Joort asked?

Why did the mirrors have an affinity for humans? Would it make a difference here?

Doing an about face he ran full sprint to the other side of the arena, beneath the sight of the paramani's delegation and guests. The crowd booed and jeered at him for a coward.

The sarpan took the same meaning and walked closer, in a measured, almost leisurely pace.

Rory dropped his sword and took the back stance, knife hand form, holding very still, concentrating on the words, the feeling he must evoke. He supinated the knife hand so he could see the rose tattoo and meditated on it, on the grief and pain, building the sorrow in fiery darts of fire into his arm. The tattoo glowed.

He thought the word of power in his head. Destruction, in ancient Altari. He turned his palm towards the adversary.

He ran at the sarpan, did a handspring and flipped head over heels, and grabbed the pike maul's shaft with both hands as the momentum carried him and in a twisting motion wrenched the weapon out of the sarpan's hands. The maul rotated with his body on the follow through and struck the sarpan in the back, making him stagger. Down but not enough, and certainly not out of the fight.

The crowd roared in delight for the home team. The maul, too heavy to wield, he left on the sandpit and dove for the sword he had laid down and rolled to slash on the upward lunge. His left arm, the knife hand arm chilled, the tattoo going from fire hot to deathly cold, and he stumbled.

The sarpan drew a curved long knife, cruel as a scimitar, but shaped for close in fighting. Though a billion eyes across Commonwealth space watched him, he felt as if someone was watching him and he stole a glance at the champion box and saw Artemesia Zayan leaning forward murmuring something he could not hear, but he felt the world shift, unstable, probabilities shifting in the sixth sense champions had for the myriad paths of possibility that made up an uncertain and malleable future.

Rory threw the sword at the box, an unpardonable attack, except this was the Grand Arena and vendetta was in play. The paramani's guards clustered around her blocking her off from Rory's sight. A sergeant trained a beam rifle, aiming at him, but held fire, even as the sword clanged off the box just under the Zayanite's seat. She flinched back, her concentration broken.

Rory's arm warmed, fury rising as he added up events to the bleak realization that Jade had died because Zayan wanted more territory and in the Game of Knives that the houses played, wanted to destroy anyone not under their control.

He shouted at the sarpan. "Are you a slave or a dog that you cannot fight for yourself but need the aid of a human to save your worthless skin?"

It blinked.

Moments were all he had. He could not save Jade. Could he save her people? If the fight ended in a draw, the vendetta would close on itself, and the colonies would be left to the usual vagaries of politics and diplomacy, safe for now.

He imagined the tattoo on her arm in his mind's eye. A coiling serpent.

The sarpan snarled and grabbed him by his combat harness lifting him off his feet. He resisted the urge to fight it, concentrating on the Zayanite. His forearm warmed, the passion of his loss feeding the mirror tattoo.

The sarpan poised the knife tip in front of his right eye, and it took all his strength to hold it off. A scent of roses filled the surrounding air. The sarpan sniffed and shook his head. The smell, like the roses at the palace garden. Exactly like the roses, the ones he had tended since the day of his orphaning. The ones he had picked for Jade when wooing her. Grief rose like a thunderstorm howling in his soul and he spoke another word, aiming his desolation at the enemy that was responsible.

She resisted. She was a quantum champion after all, but the combat had passed all boundaries of probability into regions of chaos where anything might happen. Her sleeve burst into flame and she shuddered, and his rose tattoo spat forth lightning. Actinic light flared, the sarpan dropped him and covered its eyes falling to its knees. He fell prone, and when he looked up his enemy was gone. Pandemonium ensued. The contest was over. The colonies would be safe for now.

Only the champions with the second sight knew what had really happened. The crowd's cries gave way to murmurs of confusion. The Lady Chani called the contest over. Arena security guards took charge and led the sarpan and him away to their sections. Rory, alone with his thoughts could only mourn.

Chapter 20: The Rose in Winter

He refused all interviews and the galactic celebrity that came with such an unlikely victory over a saurian gladiator. Lady Chani gave him permission to return home until duty called him back.

On Coriander, at the palace gardens he revisited the place he had tended. Fall had arrived and all the trees had lost their leaves, a blanket of orange and gold. The rose bush was still there, growing, a single red rose left upon it before the fall of winter. He pondered in his heart the memory of Jade giving the first rose to him so long ago, to comfort him when he had lost his family the first time.

He could never look on such beauty without pain, yet he could not forget the love he had felt once that never came to bear fruit. Thorns and memory would not have been his choice of what he could save from their love. The scars on his arm from the mirror of lightning's dust reminded him that nothing disappeared without a trace. When his journey in this vale of tears was done, perhaps he would meet Jade again, but not today.

www.ingramcontent.com/pod-product-compliance
Lightning Source LLC
Chambersburg PA
CBHW030146200626
46812CB00015B/1721